IT ALL BEGINS SERIES

Changes
Vol. 3

R.g. Myers

ISBN: 9798636652281

This is the diary of Jennifer Hopkins

Moving on

We were still in the house and I was deciding whether we should move or just wait. Brad and I were together, and it was not the same for me. To him, he felt he didn't do anything wrong to end our marriage. I thought differently. Tom would occasionally say hello to me, and I knew that he cared for me. I was in my third month of pregnancy feeling as miserable as I could. I was not happy that Brad did not use protection. He swore to me that he would, and he didn't. Now I must bring another baby into the world. Brad would sit outside with the guys talking and drinking. He never gave up his drinking, the only thing he gave up was his promises. I was not happy at all. In fact, I was miserable. I couldn't do anything to change my marriage, nothing. I decided to move on after the baby was born.

Paul

I was sitting outside, and Paul asked to talk to me alone. I asked if he wanted a glass of lemonade. He accepted and so we drank our lemonade and talked. Paul said, "Jennifer, I have to tell you the truth about something I witnessed." I said, "Sure Paul, go ahead." He said, "That night when you found Brad at the bar with another woman, well I followed you. It was to make sure you were safe and nothing else. You left after what you saw and then putting your wedding ring on the dashboard. I stayed. I waited and hoped that it wasn't what you thought. It had to be two hours after that you left, and I stayed. Brad and that woman left the bar and went into his truck. He found your ring and put it into his pocket. They left. I followed them. Both went to the local motel where they took a room together. I wanted to stay longer and so I did for about an hour and it was nighttime by now. The light went off in the room and I knew what was happening." I told Paul, "No more Paul, please no more." I stood up, "I knew it and I had no proof to what I thought. Brad of course denied it and said he was with her, but not that way. Now I have proof to convict him." Paul stood up, "I am so sorry my lady for having to be the one to tell you." I thanked him with all my heart as I prepared my case with Brad.

You lied

I asked to speak to Brad and he said, "Sure, what is needed." I looked at him as I stood up, "You no good bastard, you lied to me." He looked at me, "Now at what Jennifer?" I said, "You and that woman you were with at the motel. You had a one-night stand with her at that motel outside of town." Brad looked at me, "Alright Jennifer, you caught me red handed, yes I did." I fell on the chair, "Then you had nerve to had relations with me getting me pregnant after you had relations with that woman. You are disgusting Brad. Your brother never did that to me." He asked what he should do. I said, "Get the hell out of her Brad for good. Go find that woman that you had that fling with and live with her." He packed his suitcase taking his items. He kissed Clara and told me that he was sorry. I said, "There is no sorry for someone who lied with a stranger over his wife." Brad left and I heard his truck starting. I sat on the edge of the bed as I cried. I was never so mad at what he did to me. As an attorney, one must need proper evidence before convicting anyone. I had no evidence against Brad, only what I saw. Paul had the evidence to give to me and therefore Brad was convicted and punished. I am divorced from him as I sent those papers to Los Angeles hoping they received them. I turned off the light and I went to sleep praying to God for help and comfort.

The scanner tells it all
The scanner was plugged in and I sat there trying to reach anyone for information. Nothing. I told Jack and the others, "Leave it on and when someone comes on, please talk and call me." Jack agreed and so I sat outside by myself. I was crying on and off because of Brad and Melinda came out with Grace. Both told me that they would support me. I told them that was nice of them. I was sitting outside, and the scanner went off. Jack ran to get me and so I went inside. Jack was on the scanner with a woman from the Los Angeles area. Jack asked how it was and she said, "Bad. We are in the house and not allowed to go out." I knew that things were not good, and I forgot the idea of even returning to my home. I went

back outside, and I put my head down. I was not happy, my marriage blew up in my face, I am pregnant and now I have nothing to say. I was sitting outside alone, and then Brad came back as he ran up to me. He was yelling and I told him to calm down and tell me. He said, "Jennifer, I was riding outside of town and there was a younger woman who resembled you. In fact, I thought it was you and so I stopped." I asked where he saw this woman. He said, "Over by Grant Street." I asked if he could take me over to that street so I could see. He said, "I could." I told Melinda that I was going to do something with Brad, and she looked, "Oh he is back." I said, "No, nothing like that." I asked her to watch Clara until I return. She said, "Sure thing."

Clara ran to me, "Mama." I picked her up kissing her. I left with Brad in his truck to see who this mysterious woman was.

It is her

I asked Brad what she looked like. He said, "Jennifer, like you. How else could I describe her?" I said, "Alright, calm down Brad." He rode over the bridge to the back road where he took me to Grant Street. He parked in front of the house that he saw the woman. I told him, "You stay here and wait." I got out and walked up the steps as I rang the bell. I waited and I heard footsteps and then the door opened. I looked at the woman and I immediately knew it was my daughter, Samantha. She looked at me, "Mother!" I hugged her and she did the same. I asked if it was really her and she said, "Yes, it is mother." She recognized that I was pregnant and asked if I wanted to sit down. I told her that would be nice and as she was closing the door, she noticed Brad sitting in the truck. She asked if that was my husband. I said, "Yes, that is Brad." She waved him inside and he came to the door. I introduced Samantha as my daughter. He looked at her, "Oh my God, I am sorry, but I never knew." I told him, "Well now you do." Samantha said, "I live here with two other women and we were about to move." I asked where, "She said, "That was the problem." I told her, "Listen, I could use extra help and your father is with us." She said, "My dad is there, oh wow mother." I told her that Chris would be so happy to see her. So, she told her friends, they packed, got into their cars and followed us. I asked before we left about Carrie and she said, "Carrie lives closed by and she is now twenty-one." I asked if she could take me. She agreed.

Carrie

Brad asked me about Samantha, and I told him that she was daughter of Chris and me. He said, "Oh, I didn't know that." I told him, "Well now you know." I told him to follow my daughter and so he did. We came to a small place and Samantha told me, "That is where she lives." I went to the door hoping she was home. I rang the bell, and someone was coming and then opened the door. Carrie looked at me, "Mother, this is not really happening." I said, "Yes, it is, and I found Samantha too." She hugged me and I asked how she was doing. She said, "I am fine mother." I told her to get her things and come with us. She said, "Let me get my things." She packed what she could and left with us. I hugged her again and asked her to follow us. I got back into the truck and Brad looked at me. I told him, "Take us home." He looked at me, "Who is she now?" I said, "My other daughter, Carrie." He said, "I can't believe this Jennifer." I said, "You don't have to believe anything, just keep your mouth quiet." We rode home and Brad was permitted to stay, but not in the same bedroom that I was in with Clara.

Surprise Chris!

I went inside and I asked Chris to come outside. He asked if I was alright. I said, "I am fine." I told him as he came to the door to close his eyes. He did. Then Samantha came up to him and I told him to look. He did and he started to yell out, "My God, my daughter!" They both hugged one another, and I left them alone. I took Carrie inside as I introduced her to most who didn't know who she was. Brad put his things in the corner and claimed the floor with his sleeping bag. He sat with his mother and aunt.

Telling the story
I explained to Samantha and Carrie that after that earthquake and I was back at my mansion, I noticed that they were not. I didn't know where to go or where to look. I was not even sure where they lived or even existed. Samantha understood and so did Carrie. I told them that I missed them

so much and that I was the happiest mother around. I went to Brad thanking him that he found my daughter. I told him he could stay, but we are no longer a couple. He said, "I understand Jennifer." I thanked him again and we waited for dinner to be called.

The answer is clear

Brad came up to me asking if we could get back together again. I said it clearly to him, "No!" I told him not to waste his breath anymore because I was not interested. I went to sit down, and Paul said that he would send out Peter and Isoo to scout. I told him to go ahead. I wasn't sure what was happening out there, but I was sure something was. Brad was talking to Al and I was sure it was his way of crying the blues about me. I did not want Brad back. I had enough and this was the wrong time for him to do what he has done. I decided to move on in my life without him. His mother and aunt agreed with me and so I told them to keep an eye on Clara in case we are attacked. They agreed with me and so I sat down waiting for Peter and Isoo to come back.

Lockdown and attacks
The area was locked down by the military. I have not seen any sign where they were, but I was sure they were in the town somewhere. Peter came back with Isoo and they both told me, "The military locked down the entire area and we were not able to leave. Zombies are coming in on the opposite side of where the military is positioned." I took out my

map and I looked. I asked Peter where and he pointed, "There!" I looked, "No, this is near us and if I am right in what I am hearing from you, they are not far from us." Isoo nodded and I said to everyone, "Hurry up an prepare, they are on their way!" I told Paul to gather the warriors and wait. All the guys on the major weapons went outside to prepare. I put on my gear and I went outside too. Brad came to me saying that I needed to not fight. I told him to get inside or fight. I walked away. Tom was near me and he said that he would help me. I thanked him. The sun was blazing, and my sunglasses was hot from being in the sun. I watched and I knew that my binoculars were not lying to me when I saw a group of them coming to us.

The attack is now
I gathered everyone and my daughter
was with Carrie with their rifles. I told
them to be careful and they both said,
"Mother, we are ready." I smiled and
we waited. I looked at my watch and
it was 1:34PM. Then they appeared.
Paul and the warriors positioned their
swords and I saw them charging and
I told everyone to get ready. There
came the zombies coming at us. Al
was setting them on fire and so the
cannon was shot right in the middle
of the group. I told Tom that I was
moving towards the back and he said,
"I will watch and have you covered."
I then moved towards the wooded
area so they would not see me firing
at them. I moved backwards as I
positioned myself and then my foot
slipped, and I didn't know that there

was a steep step and I went down as I rolled downward. I was screaming and no one heard me because of the rifles and cannon being fired. I lied there as I could not move my leg. I was bleeding and I already knew that I lost the baby. I was hurting in all areas of my body. I tried to get up and I couldn't. My face was scratched, and I had pebbles in my mouth and hair. The dust was covering my clothes as I lied there in pain.

My rescue

I was trying to get up and it was useless. Then I heard Tom, "Jennifer, where are you?" I yelled with every breath I had, "Tom, here, help me!" He looked downward from where I was and said, "Oh my God, hold on I will come down to get you." It was far down for him to jump but easier to climb back up. He jumped down and there he asked if I was hurt. I said, "Yes, I am." He picked me up and said, "Hold on, I will help you up." Tom was strong and he held me as he got me up the steep cliff. He picked me up even more and then went passed the rifles, and all the other weapons firing. He took me in the house and called for Dora. Dora ran over, "Oh my God!" I looked at Dora, "I lost the baby." I wanted to cry, and I couldn't. Dora asked Tom if he was able to help her. He said, "Of course I was a medic in the army." She examined me having Tom cleaning off my wounds. I told her my leg was hurting badly. She examined it asking, "Isn't this the one that you hurt when you fell in the snow?" I said, "Yes, and that is why it is hurting." Tom was cleaning my face and hands as I was watching him. He smiled as he was cleaning my wounds and I was grateful he found me. Dora was examining me and saw I was bleeding and said, "I know you lost the baby." She gave me an injection and I fell asleep. I had no idea what happened to me after that.

Waking up

I woke up and I am not sure how I was doing. Dora was on the side of me and Tom was on the other side. I looked at both and Dora said, "You are going to be alright." I nodded. Then she said, "I am sorry, but we had to take the baby out and he was dead Jennifer." I told her that I did not want to hear it and to let me know about my other injuries. She said, "You didn't break anything, just sprained your leg with cuts and bruises." I thanked her. Tom was crying and I told him not to. It was not the first time, but I could guarantee it was the last. I was told to rest. Tom brought me soup and tea, and then he fed me. I asked why he was doing all of this for me. He smiled, "I was a medic in the army for all those years and not one did I not help. I am certainly not beginning with you." I tried smiling and I couldn't. I asked Tom if he told Brad and he said, "Dora did." I told Tom I did not want to see Brad. He said that Dora took care of that. I was through with Brad, I truly was. I finished my soup and tea, then I went back to sleep. I was sure that Tom would stay by my side until I would wake up.

The fight

I woke up by hearing a fight and screaming. I got up the best I could hopping with my crutch. I saw Tom and Brad fighting. Brad was yelling at Tom and ready to hit him. I yelled down, "Damn it Brad, stop it!" I got to the bottom step as I leaned on my crutch. I looked at Tom and his mouth was bleeding. Brad said, "You let him help you." I told Brad, "We are divorced, and you need to leave, or I will take my rifle and shoot you down without thinking twice. I was angered by Brad. I asked Tom who started it and he said, "It wasn't me Jennifer, it was Brad. He was upset that I was with you. He didn't know that I was a medic helping Dora." I went up to Brad, "You and your jealousy, take it and leave." I sat down with the girls and my daughters. Samantha told me to rest. I was bleeding and Dora told me that I needed to rest for a week so I would not hemorrhage." Jack and Tom helped me upstairs and put me into the bed. I was never so upset and depressed over my life.

Crying over life

I prayed so hard, repenting of what I thought and did. I was never so upset over my marriage to Brad. I was deeply hurt because I gave him everything, I had of me. I even gave him millions of dollars to help him, and he turns around and sleeps with another woman. I was not sure how old the woman was, but what if she becomes pregnant, then what? I cried and cried until my eyes were damped by tears. My baby was dead, and I needed to give up my position as leader. I told God it was over and that I wanted to turn it over to my daughters, Samantha and Carrie. I called both girls up and I told them how I felt and why. I told both, "I will be like the back burner watching and helping you, but not leading." My daughter Samantha said, "Mother, I can help, but I am not fit like you to lead." I replied, "What you do if I died then what?" She looked at me, "I understand. Fine mother both Carrie and I will lead and listen to what you say." I said, "Good, I can rest now. Now go ahead and tell the group and let me rest for a week and then I will help you in what you need." They both hugged me and left. I was contented and I needed to take myself away from it and rest.

Getting back

I finally got out of bed as I had to exercise my leg. My bleeding stopped as I prayed. I felt better and Dora examined me. She took Tom as her assistant and told me that she would take care of him for me. I smiled. Tom was good to me and I loved him in my own way, but not enough to have a relationship with him. I wanted him to be special to me like anything in my life. I didn't want it to be ruined by falling in love or having a relationship. I cherished my friendship with Tom and if it wasn't for him saving me again, I would have never been alive. No one knew where I was, and he found me. I told Samantha that I was feeling much better and I asked how she was doing. She said, "I am doing good and I had Peter and Isoo scout for me." I said, "That is good and what happened?" She said, "Nothing, we are cleared." I walked over to the door as I went outside. I asked where the bodies went and Paul came over, "My lady, we piled them up in the back and burned their bodies." I thanked him. I went outside to get sun and air as I walked slowly with my crutch. My leg was a bit weak, but it was healing. I went over to my truck as I opened the window. It was hotter than hot inside and so I wanted to take a ride, but then I said no to myself. Instead I sat on the porch praying silently. Melinda came out with Clara as my baby ran to me, "Mama." I picked her up and kissed Clara. She asked me where dada was and I told her, "He had to go somewhere." I asked Melinda if Brad left. She said, "Yes he did. My son messed up everything." I said, "Unfortunately he did." Melinda said, "He had a lot of problems with his first wife. I didn't want to tell you, but he basically did the same to her." I asked what that might be. She said, "He drank, but not much. Now Lori was not a drinker, but Brad was. He never cheated on her, and one day she had enough and left him. She divorced him after a year of marriage." I said, "I guess Brad did not learn his lesson." She said, "I am afraid not." I told Melinda that I would always love Brad, but Don was special to heart. I made it a point to tell her that I did not think any lesser about Brad than Don. She understood. I put my head down as I fell such an emptiness in my heart. Tom came out as I looked at him. He asked if I was feeling alright. I said, "I am fine. Just sitting here talking to Melinda." He said, "Well Dora was concerned." I looked at Tom, "I guess you weren't." He said, "Me too." He smiled and went inside. Melinda asked if I liked Tom. I said, "He is only a good friend and nothing more."

The question rises Samantha was telling me about Peter and Isoo going out spying and I asked if they came up with anything worthwhile. She said, "Yes, we are trapped." I asked for her to explain. She said, "We cannot get out of California because the military put walls around this area, and we are trapped inside." I said, "No way, there has to be some way for us to get out, like a back road to Oregon." She said, "I am not sure mother, but I think I am going to let Peter and Isoo find that out for us." I told her that would be wise to do so. I went back inside as I sat down. Everyone was talking and some were cleaning their rifles. Carrie was socializing with Daniel the soldier. I knew that she was a bit younger than he was. What could I do about it? Maybe they will be friends like Tom and me. Tom came over to me bringing me a cup of tea. He said, "Here Jennifer, I am sure this will soothe you." I smiled, "I thank you Tom." He said, "You are welcomed." Doris asked if I liked Tom. I said, "I like him as a friend and nothing else." She smiled, "I know you for years and been with you for many of the missions, and I saw when you had an interest in someone. This time is no different." I smiled, "I guess not."

Making plans to leave

We had to get out of California and there was no way now we could. Chris said, "Jennifer, I will help Samantha and Carrie." I told him that would be good. I knew I had to get out and see what was around. So, I went out to my truck and took a ride. Phyllis went with me. I told her to keep her rifle on her lap. We rode about two miles down and the walls were up. I went to the wall and I investigated. There was no way we could go pass it. I was furious. Phyllis asked if there was another way to Oregon. I said, "I am not sure at all." Then I thought, "Yes, there is, and it will take time." She asked what. I said, "If we go back to Los Angeles, then through San Diego and Baker, then into Nevada, you know the route." She said, "Yes, but we have to go so many miles and hours." I told her, "Well, it is either being shut here or move on." We got back into the truck and went home to tell everyone.

Jack tells it all

We went back home, and I told Samantha and Carrie what was happening. Then Jack heard and he asked if we could take the back road to Oregon. I told him, "I was hoping you would know." He said, "I know California and Oregon from the back hand." I said, "Then lead us." I gave him my map and so he looked at it since it had all the roads and highways. He studied it for a good hour and then he wrote down where to go. I asked if he found a route to get out. He said, "I think, but I am not sure Jennifer." I told him the best for us would be to back track to Los Angeles and go the way we went from San Diego. He said, "We could, but how would we know if it was blocked?" I said, "We wouldn't." Jack said that he would go down to the back road and it would take him perhaps two hours to find it. I said, "Then you need to take a few of us to go." Samantha said, "Mother, you can go with Jack and I will take care of the group here." I said, "That would work." It was noon and so if we would leave now, we would be in Oregon around 4:00PM. We took Chris and Tom and the rest stayed back. I understood we could be stopped, but that was not certain. We left taking our weapons and there was no one around.

To Oregon

Jack took his truck where the muffler was enough to make noise to wake up the zombies, and he had those spikes on his grill from when Shawn put them on. So many memories. We talked all of us and Tom sat with me in the back. He asked how I was feeling. I said, "Much better than I was." He nodded. I asked how he was, and he said, "I am fine." I wasn't sure what to say to him and so I just sat there as I watched. We rode down dirt roads and then we started to come to small towns and then we kept riding. Jack said, "See Jennifer, no military or walls, just the back roads." I nodded, "I could see that."

Jack asked what part of Oregon we were going to stay. I said, "I am not sure Jack. Actually, you know I turned this over to my daughters." He said, "I know that, but neither don't want it. They told us." I said, "I don't either." Jack asked me why not. I said, "Because in every mission it ruined my life and family. My marriages ended and left me with nothing." He said, "I know that feeling." I said, "I am sorry Jack." He smiled, "I know that Jennifer." Tom said, "Jennifer, give yourself a chance and not to think ahead of anything." I thanked Tom for his encouraging words. I told Jack that I am just coming back to myself after losing my baby and being severely injured. Jack understood. Chris wanted to know if I needed any help. I said,

"Perhaps later, but for now please ask your daughter." We got to the breaking point as the sign said, "Oregon." I looked around and said, "Well this is perfect." Jack said, "Yes, this is my territory." I laughed, "Yeah, your territory." I thought of Brad being part of this territory and how I missed him. He has been away for some time and that is not like him. I guess he got the message and left.

Looking to leave

We went back home after a bit on the road. I told everyone that we had hope and Oregon was before our face. I told Samantha and Carrie to make plans to leave the following day in the morning. So, we packed everything, and the warriors put their suitcases and gear into the trucks. We had a quick dinner, then to sleep.

Leaving California

We left the house and it was raining. It was the worse day to do anything. I knew that we had no choice, but to get out of California. Jack was leading the convoy. We were riding and then to the corner of my eyes in the wooded area was Brad's truck. I pulled to the side as everyone stopped. I got out and there I ran to it as I was not sure what I would find. Al and Jack ran behind me as the rain pounded on our heads. I was afraid in what I would find and so I opened the door and there was Brad unconscious. I screamed for Dora and Tom and they came running. Dora climbed into the truck while Tom took the other side. She said, "He is alive, but drunk. I am not sure how much he had, but he is injured."

I looked at the truck and he crashed it into the tree. I asked Dora what we should do. She looked at me, "We have to go back to the house. There is no way he is going to make it out here." I stood there as I looked at Samantha. She said, "Let us go back mother." I put my head down, "Damn it Brad." We turned around and Samantha told Paul to take in only what we needed as I sat on the sofa. Dora and Tom were taking care of Brad. His mother was by his side as she knew that this was not the first time for him to have done this. I wished she would have told me about Brad and then I would have said nothing about marriage. I sat on the sofa as depressed as I was. I looked at Samantha, "I hope we could leave by the weekend." She said, "Mother, we are fine here until he gets better." I looked at her, "Yeah, I guess so." I really had no feelings for Brad and if he got better, that was fine, not for me, but for himself. I was tired of him being drunk and doing these stupid things. Now he is without a vehicle. I was not happy about him taking the team down to nothing. I just shut my mouth letting Samantha take care of the group. What else could I do? The rain was coming down in buckets and it reminded me of when Don and I were in the flood. I was sorry for tragedies and this one now adds into the sorrow. I told Melinda, "He is your son, and you decide what has to be done with him. I am no longer his wife and I cannot let him take me down anymore." She understood.

Brads comes to it

Brad came out of his drunkenness and I said nothing to him. I was not saying a word to him. He looked at me as he was hurt from the accident. He tried getting up and so his mother took care of him. Dora would help him and Tom, well he asked if I was alright from what was happening. I said, "Of course I am. I am more worried about leaving here and being trapped than Brad." Tom nodded. I got up as my leg was hurting. It only has been a few weeks since I was hurt, and I had to adapt to what was surrounding me. I knew since Brad was hurt was his fault, first for drinking, and secondly driving. I bit my tongue as I wanted to tell him off so badly. I didn't want him in the group and that was the final decision.

I told Samantha that was my wishes and not to hold it against me. She said, "Mother, this is your group. I am not interested in it as much as you want me to be." I looked at her, "Then you want me to lead it?" She said, "Yes. Carrie and I discussed it and we both agreed to give it back to you." I told her, "I love you and Carrie and fine I will." I took back the leadership and I told Brad to his face, "You are not coming with us to Oregon." He said, "Jennifer, I have no vehicle." I said, "Well then you should have thought of that when drinking and crashing." I walked away as I told Paul and Isoo to go out and scout. I was becoming itchy and I knew that I was going to have to get him a vehicle so he could leave. I had no other choice what to do.

Al does it all

Al and Jack went to find Brad a truck. He was doing better and all he had was a few cuts over his forehead with a busted lip. Brad wanted to get back with me and I told him, "No, we are divorced and if you ask me one more time, I will have you removed." He looked at me, "Alright Jennifer." I told him that he would have to find something or shut his mouth. Jack and Al came back with a black truck for Brad. I never asked them where they got it from. I could only imagine. Brad got out of bed going outside to see the truck. I told him that he better keeps his things in the truck. He said, "All my things are at my old truck." I told him to take his new truck and go to his old one and get his belongings.

He got dressed and went to his old truck. His mother and aunt went with him to make sure he was alright. I told the others, "We leave tomorrow morning." I had a small dinner and I was not myself since I lost my baby. I still hurt, that is my leg and falling on it twice in a row, well that did not make it healthy. Dora came over to me, "Are you feeling alright?" I said, "I am just hurting." She asked me where and I told her, "My leg." She pushed up my pants and examined my leg. She called Tom over and he looked just as Dora was doing. Both agreed that I had to rest and the pressure on the leg was allowing the ligaments to hurt. I told Dora, "We have to leave here tomorrow and then find a place in Ashland." She looked at me, "Well then Jennifer you have to be off your leg. You haven't been off it much." I said, "I know, and it doesn't matter." I walked away and Tom told me, "You need to listen Jennifer." I told Tom, "I have a group to operate and nothing can stop it." Tom said, "I could." I looked at Tom, "What do you mean?" He said, "Just what I said. I care for you and I don't want to see you hurting." I looked at Tom, "Thank you." I got up and walked over to the door and there came Brad again. His truck had his belongings. I said nothing to him, and I took care of Clara. She was playing with the other babies and Sharon was with Al talking. I sat with them and it was warm. Sharon asked if we were getting out of California. I said, "I guess we are." She said, "I am patient with all of this, and I am not sure how you are feeling about it, but I wish I was not here, but in Florida with my family." I told her, "I am sure Sharon, but how can we get down to Florida with all this happening?" She said, "Do what we always did." I said, "Yeah I know that." It was horrible, but we managed to leave the following day for a new life.

Another rubble

We were taking out times going through the back roads. The road was muddy, and my truck looked as though it rolled in the mud playing. We had two hours to ride and when we were there was an earthquake that shook the entire area. We had to stop and the worse was when the trees before us fell blocking our view. We could go nowhere. We stayed in our vehicles until the earth stopped shaking. Phyllis had Clara and I asked if she was alright. She said, "She is fine Jennifer." I thanked God. After a few aftershocks, well we got out to look to see how in the world we were going to get out. Paul and the warriors were looking, and Paul said, "We will take care of that Jennifer." I asked how long, and he said, "Perhaps an hour or so." I got out to walk around and I took Clara with me. Thank God there were no trees around where we parked, or we would have had one of them fall on us. We waited and waited. All the men were helping, and we finally could move. We got back into the vehicles and went a bit more and then another problem hit us. The river that ran across was flooded. The ground before us looked as though it was a swimming pool. We could not get through to cross over to Oregon. I fell back in my seat as I threw my hands up. Jack came up to me, "I guess that idea is shot." I said, "Yes, it is." He looked around and there was no way we could get out, not with the water. Sure, we could ride our trucks through the water, but how deep it was, no one knew. I just sat there in despair as we were trapped. The damn walls had to be there so we could not get out. I told everyone, "We have to go back." Tom said we could go back to Edgewood and stay at his house. I said, "That would be nice, but the zombies are there and no wall up." We had no choice, but to go back to where we were. I was desperate and I felt like a worm crawling out of sand. We turned back and went to the house that we left a second time. Paul asked if we were to stay. I said, "I have no choice Paul. We are absolutely trapped in California. For how long, I have no idea."

Wake me up later

It was raining which did not help the matter, especially crossing over where that river was located. We were cooked and trapped. The walls were up, and I felt like I was in prison. I went to my room to lie on the bed. I just finished dinner and so did Clara. I gave her a sponge bath with new pajamas on her. She had her bottle and fell asleep. I took a shower, and then I lied on the bed as I was tired. I had no answers to the questions I had in my mind. It was either sink or swim. I felt like sinking. I told God that I was heart stricken and that I had a drunken husband, nowhere to go, trapped, and running out of food. I fell asleep praying that sirens would not ring or an earthquake.

Searching

Life was turning to survival. We had to survive and either way we went, there was a price to pay. I sent out two scouts to find a store nearby so we could get out. We had stores, but the military put up that damn wall leaving us with nothing. How stupid of them to do that. They left and I waited. Samantha came to me saying, "I am glad I gave the job back to you mother." I said, "Thank you." It seemed that everything was piling up on us. We had no way out, no food, or hope. I prayed and prayed for some miracle to happen. I told God I was discouraged, and he said, "Come on Jennifer, you are that close." I didn't know where I was closed to, but I would surely find it. Peter and Isoo came back after being away for a while. I asked the progress and Peter said, "No zombies, but there is a shopping center about three miles down the road." I asked if it was opened. Peter said, "Yes it was." I asked if the military was around. He said, "Not that I could see." I told both to get a drink and relax. I asked for volunteers to come with me to get food. Doris, Tom, Jack, and Al wanted to come. The rest would watch. I told Samantha, "Like it or not, you are in charge with your father." Chris smiled.

Food supply

There were utility men on the road fixing what the earthquake tore up. Trees were down and so we were able to get around. We found another store and so we went inside. I told Jack that we needed to get what was an emergency usage for us, and not luxury items. He laughed, "Well I guess there goes my beer." I said, "Yes and that too." The store had customers and there was food around, but not much. I was not sure how long we would be able to go through this, but I was sure we would survive. I made sure we had milk, eggs and bread. Jack threw a roast in the basket and I looked. I asked him, "Are you going to roast it Jack?" He said, "Sure I could." I shook my head. I needed diapers and food for

Clara and by the time I was finished shopping, the cart was piled up high. Tom asked what we should do if we run out of food. I said, "We will pray and believe in God." Tom smiled and so I knew that we were safe. I paid for the food as the men wheeled it to my truck and then soon after we left. In the shopping center we saw pizzeria and so Al looked at me, "Well, that looks good Jennifer." I knew what he wanted and so we went into pizzeria. Al said, "I am treating." I smiled, "Well, that is good news." He told the clerk that he wanted ten mixed up pizzas. The clerk looked, "What is mixed up pizza's sir?" Al chuckled, "Well, pepperoni, cheese, sausage, cheese, you know a few here and few there." The clerk said, "I get it." So, he went to tell the owner and we waited. Al bought us drinks and so we sat there waiting for ten mixed up pizzas to be made.

Finished and done

Al paid the clerk and so we left. He took the two pizzas he bought for himself and Sharon. He said, "Sharon loves mushrooms and I bought her a pizza with just that and me a cheese." I said, "Well we have eight to choose from." He said, "Yes, and they look good too." We left the shopping center and we went back to the house. Paul and the warriors brought in our bags and gave them to Rosa and Marie. Daniel took care of the groceries with them as I announced that there would be no dinner tonight because Al bought us pizza. Everyone cheered and so we sat down and ate. Sharon was sitting with

Al as they were talking. Brad was with his mother. I felt bad for him, I really did. I just couldn't take it anymore with his drinking. He was not the same man I married and understand how I felt. I lost a baby, a husband and maybe my sanity if I didn't pray. I thought all this while eating pizza. Tom sat with Susan and that was a relief for me. Tom knew that I didn't want to start anything up with him. I had enough.

Clara's birthday

It was my daughter's birthday. I ran down to the shopping center to see what I could buy her. I looked for a cake or something so she could get her hands messy. I saw the supermarket had a bakery and I bought a cake large enough for all of us and ice cream. There were candles and I bought a stuffed animal for her with a few blocks for her to play with. I went back home and the workers on the road were directing the traffic. I was not sure what that was all about, but I was convinced it had to do with the trees down. I reached back to the house and Brad came out to help me. He said, "I am the father." I looked at him and so he took the gifts inside. I gave the cake to Rosa as I asked her to serve it after lunch for Clara. She said that she would. Clara was sitting on the floor playing and so I gave her gifts to her. She saw the bear and blocks and I kissed her. She had on her pretty pink outfit and her hair in ribbons. She looked at the bear, "Mama bear." I said, "Yes, bear." Brad sat next to Clara, "Daddy loves you Clara." She hugged him as I wanted to cry. I put my head down to avoid my tears. I sat down with Doris as I asked about Gina. She said, "Her birthday passed when we were fighting." I told her that I was sorry. She said, "It is fine because I did what I could and that was to keep her safe." Tyrone was playing with Gina and I asked how old she was now. Doris said, "Gina is older than Clara which would make her sixteen months old." We talked for a while and then Rosa told us that she had the sandwiches and everything else on the table. We went as I held Clara's hand. I told her, "Look sweetie you have a small sandwich to eat." She looked, "Mama, where is daddy?" I said, "Somewhere." I looked for Brad and he was gone. I think he left.

The surprise

We were singing "Happy Birthday" to Clara and I turned around and there was Brad. I looked at him and he smiled. Then Clara sat down, and she had a small piece of her cake and ice cream. Brad came over to Clara, "Happy Birthday honey." He gave her a gift and I looked, "Oh my, what is it Brad?" He said, "A doll set." It was in a big box and he said it was especially for Clara. I smiled at him as he sat next to her playing. I sat on the sofa and Melinda said, "You see there is hope in him." I said, "I never said that. He has to get help for his drinking." Melinda said, "I know he does, but where at this time?" I told her that I wished I knew. She then asked if I was thinking on going back with Brad. I told her, "Not any sooner." I may be nice and talking to him, but our relationship is finished. In fact, my entire love life reached its toll. We may speak, but that is as far as it will go. I didn't take away Brad's privilege not to be with Clara, it was only with me.

Not much left

Weeks went by and we had to find something to survive. Our food supply was getting low and I did not think we would be here this long. The walls were still in front of us and I wanted to blow them up to get through to Oregon. I was sure the back road was still flooded and there was no way we could get to Ashland. Jack said, "Jennifer, I am going to take a ride to see if that area is still with water." I told him, "Jack, even if it wasn't, it would take a while for it to dry up and the ground to be solid. You know that." He said, "It only has been two months." I said, "Yes, and we need to give it at least another month then we will attempt another try. This time I will send out the scouts to check it." He agreed.

Brad is sick

Dora told me that Brad was sick. I asked what happened and she said, "He is withdrawing from alcohol." I said, "Well he needs to or this time we will find him dead." Dora and Tom took care of Brad and helped him with his withdraws. I stood away as they put him into another room. I could do nothing about it and so I did what I could do. That was to wait. Tom was nice to Brad regardless how he treated him. Tom told me that Brad was really getting nasty and it would take time to get where he should be. I said, "That is for sure." He asked if I would go back to Brad. I said, "Everyone thinks it is because of his drinking. That played a part, but what was the worse, he broke the marriage by sleeping with that woman. That is the damage." He understood. I told Tom that I was going for a walk. Clara ran after me, "Mama, me too." I picked her up, "Come on sweetie, let us go for a walk." It was nice outside and the sun was shining. I was showing Clara the flowers and butterflies. Then I picked her holding her. I hugged her as she did the same. We walked around for a while and then we came back as we sat on the porch together. Clara looked at me, "Mama, bear." I told her to come with me so I could get the bear. I walked inside as everyone was looking at me. Melinda and Grace were crying, and I asked what happened. Dora came up to me, "Brad is dead." I asked, "I was not gone more than an hour and he was alright when I left." She said, "Yes, but he killed himself Jennifer." I fell on the ground, "No, he wouldn't do that. Oh my God, he died without God." I started to cry as Tom picked me up. I said, "I want to be alone, please." Paul asked if he should bury Brad. I said, "Yes, do whatever." I couldn't see his body and so the warriors took care of him for me. I was not myself and I fell into deep depression. I had to leave the house and I told everyone, "We have to go." We packed everything as I went to Brad's grave and I told him that he was foolish in what he did. I couldn't believe it. I was in nothing, but denial and my life were literally ruined.

Going to Ashland

We left that day to cross the back roads to Ashland. The river was dried, and we passed Brad's truck as I could not bear to look at it. I had to get passed the truck, mud, and memories. Phyllis asked if I needed her to drive. I said, "No, I am fine." As soon as we would settle down, I was giving up my position to whoever wanted to lead the group. What happened to Brad was the icing on the cake for my life. I had a daughter to take care of and she was all I had left of Brad. I rode through the backroad and we finally came to the highway in Oregon. I didn't want to stay at the house because of

remembrance of Brad being there.
We managed to find an abandoned
house that once had a couple. They
left behind their pictures and things. I
was hoping they were happy together.
We settled in after a rainstorm and so
I made the announcement for the last
time that I was giving up my position
and that it was opened to whoever
wanted it. I was honest and told them
that my life ended when Brad died,
and that I had a child to raise. I went
to the porch to sit as I stared in
space. I was not myself and I rather
would have had Brad leave and die
somewhere else not knowing what
happened to him. My entire heart was
broken. Melinda was down and so
was Grace. They were crying still, and
I told them that I was not myself and
the time I had with Brad was

precious. I finally realized that I was now alone without love or Brad.

Jack and Al

Both Jack and Al took over the group. I was happy they did. Matthew and Tyrone helped them out with what they needed. I stood to the side as I would sit alone and play with Clara. Tom would come over to talk to me and I said, "It is no use Tom, my life is shattered." He said, "I know the feeling. When my wife cheated me, divorce and took the children, I was shattered. I know it is not the same, but pain is pain. It never changes. I am here for you, always remember that." I thanked him. I went inside the cabin and I congratulated both Jack and Al. I told them that I knew they would do a good job. Jack hugged me, "I am sorry Jennifer." I told him not to be. I smiled and walked away. There was nothing to do and so I went outside. Jack came out telling me that there was a facility around Ashland and that he wanted me to come so they could get rations. I said, "No, I am done right now. Take someone else besides me." I went to my truck and I sat in there for a while listening to music. I wiped my eyes a thousand times and blew my nose even more. No one had to tell me about how Brad died, I knew he shot himself because from the distance I heard a gunshot when I was out with Clara. That is why I walked back. I kept it a secret from everyone that I knew the truth. It was part of my life, secrets, and hope for the future. I had to move on in my life, and maybe leave the group and find hope somewhere rather than running. I was done with all of it. I had to just plan it and then do it.

Calling on God

Dora and Tom were concerned about my mental health. I laughed, "I am not." I would stay in my room alone as I would pray. I had nothing else than what I had with God. I told God I wanted to leave the group and make it on my own with my daughter. Of course, God did not say anything to me. He was quiet and that told me I was permitted to do what I felt like. I looked at my map and I thought of going back to Henderson, but then I would have to deal with Shawn. I wasn't sure where to go. I thought this out for days, and sometimes weeks until I found where to go. I packed my suitcase and Tom came in to see me with dinner. He asked where I was going. I told him since he was good to me. I said, "I am leaving the group and going on my own with Clara." He looked at me, "You mean you are leaving without me." I said, "Of course." He put his head down, "Well that is not fair to me. I care for you Jennifer, even though you don't." I said, "I cannot comment on that one." He said, "I know, I know." He stood up from the bed, "I am going with you and we could live separate lives, but at least I will know you are safe." I told him, "Suit yourself." He asked when and I told him, "Tomorrow." He promised to have his suitcase ready and that he would go when I would. I told him again, "Suit yourself." I had my dinner and then I got Clara ready for bed. I went to sleep hoping my life would be better.

                    Leaving for Cottage Grove
I said goodbye to everyone in my group and my daughters wanted to come because they said we were apart for a while. I told them that would be nice. I wished the rest the best and Tom got into his truck and said goodbye to Dora. He promised her that he would take care of me. I laughed on the way. My daughter took their cars and followed me to Cottage Grove. On the way we stopped at a restaurant. We had another hour to ride. Tom got out of his truck and met me at mine. He asked if he could eat with us. I said, "Sure, of course." My daughters were helping me, and Tom was nice

enough to take Clara. She was playing with his face as I smiled. At one point she called him Daddy and I wanted to cry. Tom assured me that it was alright, and that Clara didn't know. We sat down in a booth as the waitress gave us the menu. I decided to have a cheesesteak and a coke. The waitress asked if I needed a highchair. I said, "That would work." She brought it to us, and Tom put Clara inside. The rest ordered their food and I thought that Clara would like macaroni and cheese. I gave her a bottle and she was happy. I stared out the window as though something was going to attack us. Carrie asked if I was alright and I told her, "I am fine, just getting over things." I was happy that I was away from the group and not leading it. It was a lot of weight on my shoulders and I knew that. Tom asked where we were going to live. I said, "Wherever Tom." I didn't care if I never was to settle down to something in my life. He asked if I was thinking of going back into practice. I put my head down, "Maybe, who knows." The food came and so I gave Clara her macaroni and cheese. She took her spoon and fed herself. I told Tom, "I love this age because she can start feeding herself." I loved my daughter and so we ate, and the waitress asked where we were going. I said, "To Cottage Grove." She said, "You will like it there. It is very quaint, and the people are nice." I told her thank you as I left her a generous tip. We got back into our vehicles as I rode with Clara. She fell asleep and so I put the music on as I finished my journey to Cottage Grove.

Arrival

We arrived in Cottage Grove and indeed the town was quaint. I parked and then I saw a familiar truck parking near Tom. Samantha ran up to her father, "Dad." I looked and it was Chris. He hugged me and his daughter. Tom put his head down and I smiled. Chris said, "I followed you because of my daughter. I didn't want to lose her again." I agreed to that. Tom asked where we should stay. I looked around as we walked, "There is a small hotel, maybe we can get rooms there." We agreed and walked over. Chris was happy that he had his daughter and so Carrie walked with me and Clara. Tom was with me too. We arrived at the hotel and it was small. The gentleman welcomed us, and he asked how he may help us. I said, "Well, we are looking for a few rooms." He asked how many and I said, "Four would do." He asked if I would like the family room for me and my daughter and husband. I said, "No, it is only me and my daughter." He smiled, "Sure, I can accommodate all of you. How many nights would you like?" I said, "I am looking for a place to rent or buy." He said, "Well I own a few cottages about a mile out. Stick around and I can help you out." I thanked him. I paid for everyone for two nights and hopefully after that we would have a place to stay. He said, "Here is your keys and we have a small restaurant right around the corner. It closes at 8:00PM."

Invitation

Tom invited me to dinner, and I refused. I told him that I already went there and ordered out sandwiches and something for Clara. He felt bad, but he understood. I told him that I wanted to rest since I was tired. He said that he understood. I told him to enjoy his dinner and that I would see him in the morning. I closed the door and I went to take a bath. The room was nice and quaint. I put Clara down to sleep and so I had the television on and my bath running. I was exhausted from riding and all the emotions I have been through. I felt bad for Tom, but I was not ready or will be for another relationship. I was well down and so I took a warm bath hoping I could relax. My leg was bothering me from all those crazy falls. I thought to mention something to Tom in the morning. I finished my bath and I combed my hair after spraying a fragrance of roses on my hair. I got into bed and watched television. Nothing about zombies and I was happy about that. I went to sleep soon after and I prayed for all my friends that I left behind. I also prayed for who was with me and a new place to live.

Living again

I spoke to the owner and he told me that he had several cottages that would fit all of us. I said, "Well, that would be good." He gave me directions and said, "Here is the key to the one I think you would like." I GPS it and I went with Clara. She was playing with her bear. It wasn't far at all and nestled right into a community. I was happy about that. I was tire of having no one around. I found the cottage and it was large enough. I got out and I held Clara and she pointed to the house. I said, "Yes, a new home for us." I opened the door and it was furnished. Very nice looking. It had a fireplace, a large kitchen and living room. I went upstairs as it had five bedrooms. Pretty alright. I looked in the back and the view caught my breath. I knew this was my home, for at least for a while. I went back to see the owner and I asked how much. He said, "I can give it to you for $850 a month and a month security." I took the money out of my purse and put it on the desk. He looked. I said, "Don't worry I am a lawyer from California." He smiled, "I knew you were something." He wrote out the receipt and I was paid for a month. His name was Charlie and he gave me the key. I thanked him as we were ready to leave. He called me back, "Here is your change Miss Hopkins." I looked and asked, "What change?" He said, "Your leaving and I am refunding for today." I smiled, "Thank you."

Moving out

We arrived at the cottage which was nice. Everyone loved it and so we settled down until we needed food. Chris asked Tom to come with him while I rested. I asked where they were going and Chris said, "We will be back." I looked at the girls and they smiled. Clara was playing on the floor and the cottage had a lot of sunlight. Something I craved for. I went to the back porch and it was nice. The air was fresh, and I always loved Oregon. It was always special to me with my missions. I sat there looking at my watch and it was over an hour since they left. Carrie told me, "Mother, they are fine. There are no zombies here." I smiled as I knew she was right.

Coming back

Chris and Tom came back, and they went shopping for food in which they had so many bags of food. They also stopped at a fast food for us. I thanked both as they put the food away and our refrigerator was packed along with our cabinets. We had burgers and fries. I was enjoying my chocolate shake. I gave a small portion to Clara as she could chew. She had some with her milk and smiling as she was chewing. I laughed. I told everyone that I was well satisfied with my new life. Chris asked me why I left. I said, "I had to or else I would have had a breakdown. Right now, I am still recuperating from the loss of Brad. It will take time as you know." He nodded. I told Chris, "I am sure they will survive. They have good people in that group that could survive anywhere in the world." I wanted to cry, and so I held it back. I thanked them all again for the food and burgers. I told them that I was going to my room so Clara could get a bath. I hugged my daughters and Chris and Tom. Tom said that he would make sure everything is locked and the curtains drawn. I turned around, "You remembered."

Phyllis pleads

Today I received a call from Phyllis, and she was upset because I did not take her. I said, "Phyllis, it is nothing about you, it is about me." She said, "I understand, but we have been good friends for so long, and then you turn around and do that to me." I felt bad for her and I told her that I did not want the team back. She said, "Then take me damn it." I said, "But you don't have a car." She was upset more, "Well can't you pick me up?" I said, "No, I can't." She then got worse and said, "Then I am going back to Henderson. I will find a way. Thanks Jennifer." She hung up on me. I did not feel like traveling that far away in where I just came from. I wanted to close myself in a sardine can forgetting the world. Tom came over and asked what was wrong. I said, "Phyllis called wanting me to pick her up." Tom said, "Well you can, or I should say I will do it for you." I told Tom that he didn't have to because I want to change my life. He said, "Jennifer, you don't throw the people away that you cared for just because you want to change your life." I said, "I don't need anything." He said, "Listen, call her and tell her that I am on my way to pick her up." I called Phyllis and she would not answer. I told Tom, "Forget it, she is not answering." He waited and nothing. I tried several times and nothing. I even left a message on her voicemail and she never called me back. I told Tom to forget about it and so he did. I did not hear anything more from her.

Going out

I never heard from Phyllis again. I kept trying her number and nothing. I left it go. I went to the town to walk around by myself. I stopped in the ice cream store. There was a line which was long. There was a gentleman ahead of me and he turned around saying, "I guess everyone has the same idea." I said, "I guess so." He extended his hand, "My name is Richard. What is your name?" I said, "I am Jennifer." He said, "Well, nice to meet you Jennifer." He asked if I lived here. I said, "I just moved here from California. Well he said, "I could understand why." He was in front of me and it was his turn to get ice cream. He asked what flavor I liked, and I said, "Chocolate." He told the clerk to give him two double scoops of strawberry and chocolate. He paid the clerk and gave me my cone. I looked at him, "Well let me pay you." He said, "No, it is a welcome gift for a beautiful lady." I said, "Thank you." We went outside and sat on the bench. He asked what a beautiful woman like me was doing out alone. I said, "I am not alone, everyone is at the house including my baby daughter." He looked at me, "I am sorry, I didn't know you were married." I said, "I am, I mean I was. My husband just passed away." He took his ice cream cone and held it to the side and said, "I am so sorry to hear that Jennifer." I said, "So am I." I finished my ice cream and I told him that I had to get back home. He said, "I thank you for sitting with me." I said, "Much appreciation to for you." He smiled, "I hope to run into you again someday." I smiled and got into my truck. I thought that was nice of Richard buying me ice cream. I wondered where he lived.

Life gets better

I didn't go out much and one day Samantha sat with me asking if I was going back into law. I said, "No, I have enough money, enough of everything." She said, "Well mother you need to find a hobby." I said, "I have a hobby, sitting here." She laughed, "No mother, a real hobby." I told her, "I will think about it." Chris and Tom were working on their trucks and my daughters were bored. I said to go out and have fun. They had cars and no excuses. Carrie said, "Come on Samantha let us go shopping at the store." They both hugged me, and they left. Clara was sleeping and so I was alone. The guys were outside, and I was sitting on the sofa. I turned on television to see what was happening in Oregon. They were talking about the zombies and they were contained in Portland. I thought of Brad and his house. I felt bad that he did that to himself. I lost Don and Brad and I was unhappy I did. I promised myself that I would not date or go out. I had enough. I started to cry over Brad, and he was gone for two months. It felt like a century. I know that he was having a hard time with drinking, and if he would have been admitted to a hospital, I believe he would have been alive at this moment. I wanted to blame Dora because she was in charge. She could have put him into the hospital, but she didn't. That is why I left, because I blamed her. She was the doctor and she had every right to do anything to help him. She never tried. He shot himself with his own gun. I was sick over it, sick I lost my baby, husband, and life. I was not myself even though things were picking up for me. I didn't care about anything except raising my daughter.

Dinner

I decided to make dinner and so I made a meatloaf. It was baking and I was hungry. The girls were back from shopping and bought a lot of different things. Dinner was almost ready and so I finished the potatoes and corn. I put everything in the bowls and dishes. I let them serve themselves as I put them on the table. We all sat down as we said the Grace.

Clara was holding her bowl and wanted to eat. I told her, "Here Clara, I crushed some meatloaf and here are mashed potatoes for you." She took her bowl and was eating. I gave her milk in her sippy cup. She had potatoes on her face, and I told her that I liked her white beard. She paid no mind and continued to eat. We all started to eat, and Chris said that I made a mean meatloaf. I thanked him. We ate and the girls did the dishes for me. I sat down as lonely as I was for myself. No one knows how lonely a person is until they say something. No one has asked and so I remain silent about it.

News is dreadful

The government today announced we were going into a recession. They just didn't have enough of money to support troops in states that are battling zombies and viruses. It was simple as that. Chris looked at me, "Now what do we do?" I said, "We get as much money as we could from the ATM and use it to live on." Tom asked if we were going to stay. I said, "When things get worse, we will move out." Chris smiled, "It seems that you are still in charge Jennifer." I smiled, "No, Tom asked me a question and so I answered it. I have not declared myself as a leader." Chris nodded as he smiled to Samantha.

Looting begins

During the evening news the newscaster made an announcement that looters were out and so were the police. No one was allowed out due to the thugs making their rounds. I told everyone to get their weapons ready. Chris said, "We only have our rifles and nothing else." I said, "There has to be a military facility around here so we could get weapons." I took out my map that had everything on it except China. I looked for a military facility and there was one outside the area. I told everyone, "We will go to this tonight." Tom said, "Well, you are forgetting one thing Jennifer, and that is Clara." I looked at my daughter as she smiled. I said, "Damn it, I have no one to watch her." Carrie said, "Mother, I will stay." I asked if she was sure. She assured me that she would. I told her to keep her rifle on hand in case. Tom said, "I will stay too Jennifer, because if these hoodlums attack, how is she going to defend herself and Clara?" I was beside myself and I knew he was right, and so I agreed. I was waiting for it to get darker and beforehand we had dinner and then we left at 9:00PM.

Looting the facility

We arrived at the facility and so I parked the truck around the corner near the trees. We walked as slow as possible and I was believing I made a mistake by leaving the rest of the group back in Ashland. We went to the gate and watched, and it was closed. No one was around, as I could see. Chris took out his cutters, cutting the chain. We went inside slowly. Chris said, "We will go inside and look, and if it is cleared, I will get the truck and bring it into the depot." I agreed with him and so we went to the first door that read, "Supply

Room." Chris opened the door as it was not locked. We went inside as we had flashlights. No one was around. Chris checked the back and it was cleared. He said, "Alright Jennifer, I am going to get the truck. May I have your keys?" I handed my keys to him to get the truck. Samantha and I looked around and we took rifles and plenty of ammunition. I put the rifles and ammunition into boxes and put them out by the bay area so Chris could load them into the truck. I then saw a sign reading, "Special forces." I went inside and there were all kinds of tactical weapons and one was a flamethrower. I smiled, "This is a blessing in itself Samantha." She agreed. Then I heard Chris, "I put everything in the truck." I showed him the flamethrowers and he smiled." We took what we could and the butane tanks. I also grabbed grenades and Chris saw a bazooka. He loaded up the truck with all the weapons we needed. It was that simple. We locked the doors and then Chris said, "Let us go to the ration section." We went to the next building that had rations for the troops. Chris and Samantha loaded as many as we could take. I smiled, "Well, this is all." We got out of the yard and Chris got out and put on a new chain with a lock that he had. I asked what the soldiers were going to do to get inside. He smiled, "Just like we did, cut the chain." We left in the truck and went back to the house. Chris watched to make sure no one was following us and so we were cleared. I told Chris to put the tarp on top of the bedding of the truck so no one will see what we have. Chris and Tom brought in more rifles and ammunition, bazooka and flamethrower. I asked Chris if he knew how to use the flamethrower and he said he did. I told him, "Well this baby is yours." Tom said he knew how to fire the bazooka from when he was in the military. I told him, "Well this baby is yours." We had new rifles that were heavier and enough. We were now ready for those bastards to come and attack us.

The call

Jack made a call to me saying that the group was leaving Ashland and wanted to know where I was located. I couldn't refuse my group that I was with for so many missions. I gave him the address and he said, "I will see you in a few." Tom looked at me, "You know God knows what you need Jennifer, and this is one time you need them." I said, "I know that." I asked Tom how much he believed in God. He said, "A lot. I was a Chaplain in the Army for some time and then I left it to be a medic. When I took care of people, I would also preach." I was impressed and he said that is how he met his wife. She was also a medic and soon after in the army they were married. I asked if he missed his wife. He said, "I do, but she married someone else. It is what it is." I agreed. Then he looked at me, "Would you consider dating me?" I looked at Tom as he threw me off with the question he asked. I said, "Tom, I am not sure. Nothing against you, it is that Brad has been gone for only three months and I lost my baby five months ago. It takes time to heal, you know that." He put his head down, "I guess it does." I told him as he was walking away, "You never know what God can do." He smiled, "That is for sure."

The arrival

It was 8:00PM. Jack and the group arrived at my front step with Paul and the horses. I told Paul, "In the back and please keep it clean with them." He smiled. Melinda hugged me along with Grace as Clara ran to her grandmother. Melinda picked her up, "Well my little dumpling, you are getting bigger." I invited everyone inside and told them to find a sleeping area. Everyone said hello to me, and Jack said, "You are in charge, I had it enough." I laughed, "I am sure you did." Rosa and Marie said hello as I told them, "There is plenty of cold cuts and bread for everyone." Rosa said that she would make sandwiches for everyone. I closed the door and I looked at Jack, "Now what is the real reason why you called me?" He said, "Ashland is on strict lockdown and gave everyone a chance to leave. The looters have been really bad in town and so we had to leave." I said that they were the same here. Then Jack commented, "But at least we are all together and could take them on." I agreed. I was looking for Phyllis and there she was sitting with Susan. I went up to her, "Phyllis, I am so sorry for being like that. You should have returned my calls." She said, "I would have if I heard from you." I told her that I called her number. She asked what number and Phyllis looked, "I am sorry, but that number is not mine." I looked at it and it was Brad's. I started to cry, "I am so sorry it is Brad's number." Phyllis held me, "It is alright Jennifer, I am sorry." I told her that I was too.

Dora and Tom

The doctor and the medic were examining all of us to make sure we were healthy because of the flu going around. It turned out to be we were just fine. Dora asked how I was taking everything. I said, "Just as good as I could." She understood. I asked how Greg has been. She said that everything was fine and that he wanted to do something instead of sitting around. I knew the feeling. Tom went to see Dora and she said,

"We are still a team to help the injured and sick." He agreed and so they were talking as I went to sit down. Sandwiches and lemonade were served to everyone. Doris asked if I was doing better. I said, "I am, but I still have my bouts of crying." She assured me that I would be fine. Sharon said, "I think we should still go to Ireland." I told her that would be nice. She said, "It is still opened to us and no one has closed the airports." I asked about her father's private jet and she said, "Still available." I was thinking on that and to move to Ireland would mean a different life. I told Sharon, "Maybe we would run into red-haired zombies." She laughed, "Maybe we would." We all talked for a while and then we locked up the house for the night. Jack said that we should be on alarm. I said, "Set up the guards." I went upstairs with Clara as I prepared her to sleep." I said my prayers to God thanking him for my group again. I fell asleep as I cried again for Brad.

Broken hearts mend

I came down with Clara for breakfast and I asked how everyone was doing. They said they were fine. Rosa gave me coffee and toast. I said, "That is all I want." I haven't been eating much. Melinda and Grace took Clara and put her into the highchair where they fed her breakfast. I was grateful for them. It was a beautiful morning and the sun was shining. I went to sit on the porch with my breakfast. Jack came out, "I must say, Oregon is a beautiful state." I said, "It always was,

and good people came from here."
He saw I had tears in my eyes. Jack
sat down, "I know you are still upset
about Brad and I feel for you
Jennifer. I really do. I wish it never
happened. You must be strong and
know that God has something for
you." I smiled, "Thank you." Al came
up to Jack, "We have to look at
Tyrone's truck, something is clicking
in it." Jack excused himself and so I
sat there eating my toast and drinking
coffee. I hoped that I would feel
better soon.

The point of survival
Cottage Grove had its problems with
looters. It was not good at all and at
night we would hear the cars going by
with screams. They haven't stopped
at our house yet. We were prepared
for them and that is why we watched

the house. I told Peter and Isoo to go on a scouting journey. They left and I knew they would come back with more information for me to decide on. I was sure we had to leave the house soon. Chris asked me, "Where to go after this Jennifer?" I told him, "Probably camping out somewhere around the mountain area." Jack looked, "We need to get near water so we can bathe, drink and wash clothes." I agreed to it and so we waited. By the time the scouts came back, we were having lunch. The weather was hot, and it was a good idea to live in the mountains in the summer, but when the winter would hit, it would be treacherous for us. Our motive was to look for abandoned homes to live and survive. We had nothing else to do.

Must get out now

Peter and Isoo came back after being away long into the morning and afternoon. I asked what they found. Peter said, "In town the looters are battling the police. A lot of shooting and blood. There isn't any signs of zombies and I would say the looters are about four miles from here. There is a lot of them." Jack said, "It is time to get out now." I said, "I am sure we could take them on if they attack us." Jack said, "Sure we could, but do we want to chance our lives. You know we could be shot. They are not zombies; these are human beings who can kill us." I looked at the map, "According to the map we are not far from the mountains and so we need to leave in the morning." We all agreed and turned in for the night.

Leaving the house

I left the key under the mat and we got into our vehicles and travelled south into the mountains. We followed the signs that read, "Mountain Trails." They were outside of Cottage Grove which made it easier for us to get places. We went up the trails and there we found on the hill a lonely cabin that was large enough for all of us. I stopped and Paul got out with Jacob to search and so they did. They came out cleared and it hasn't been lived in for a while. Paul and the warriors cleaned it out while we waited and then we went inside. It had a few manmade bedrooms and a shower. It was enough to support us for a few weeks. I told Paul to keep the rations in the truck and to make sure the tarp was covering them. He agreed and so we settled down. We were on the mountain nestled in the back surrounded by trees and a stream nearby. It was hot outside and the temperatures were higher during the day and cooler at night. Paul and Jacob chopped down wood so we would have it for the fireplace. Some of us took a walk to the stream to cool our feet down, that is how hot it was for us. Sharon said, "I want to take a swim in the water." I told her to put on her bikini. She laughed, "In a stream?" I said, "I am sure Al wouldn't mind it." She said, "I am sure he wouldn't." Doris was laughing and agreed we needed to at least get our feet wet. So, all three of us went into the stream and cooled our feet down. Sharon said, "Yes, tomorrow I am coming here with my bikini." I laughed, "I can't wait to see this one."

Hunting for food

We had a radio and there was no television. Jack hooked up the scanner so we could hear what was going on. The radio would play music and then give us the news. The world was going down, and food was scarce. Jack heard it and said that he was going out to hunt for food. I asked why and he said, "So we could have extra meat." Jack took a few guys to go out and find meat. I laughed because I was not into that yet. We had enough of food, and I was not sure where he was going to store the meat. Certainly not in our refrigerator. We had no room. We waited for this hunting and when they came back, we laughed. Jack caught nothing and I told Jack, "We have to go deep into the mountains and not hanging around here." Jack said, "Go ahead and laugh." Heidi was laughing and Jack shook his head and went inside. I thought it was hysterical.

Stranger

We sat outside today and some where at the stream cooling down. I sat in the yard and I heard a car coming and I told Tom and Chris, "Someone is here." They got their rifles and the warriors stood there with their swords drawn. I got up and waited and the car parked in the front of the cabin. A man got out and a woman sat in the front. He said hello and told us that he was not here to cause trouble, but to ask for help. I asked where he was from and he said,

"Cottage Grove. The looters have been doing a lot of damages to the town and houses, and so we escaped them." I asked his name and he said, "Jerry Colin and that is my wife Susie." I asked if they had any children and he said, "No, they are all grown and living elsewhere." I looked at everyone and they gave me the okay sign. I asked if they had weapons and Jerry said, "We do, and they are in the car." I asked Dora to examined them and Rosa to give them something to eat. I sat back down as I was waiting for half the group from the stream. It was getting cloudy and I knew we were in for a storm. I asked Jerry and Susie if they had sleeping bags. Jerry said, "Come here Jennifer and I will show you what we have." He took me and Tom to the back of his car and showed me that he had a lot of different items including two sleeping bags. He grabbed the bags and went inside. I told him to find a place and so he did. Susie brought in change of clothing and Jerry was thanking me for allowing him and his wife a place to stay. I said, "You are welcome."

Storms unrest

The rain started at night and it was coming down. I had flashbacks about Don and me that tragic day of being trapped in the water. I quickly let it go and then I came back to realization. Our trucks were locked, and the windows were up. We took our chairs inside and we waited as the wind was blowing. We shut the windows and pulled down the shades as the thunder was clashing. Clara held onto my neck as I told her not to be scared and that I was protecting her. I took her to our room, and she sat on the bed. I got her pajamas on and she wanted to sit on my lap. I told her she could. I held her to my heart as she was part Brad and I missed him so much. I was not myself although others told me to heal, I will never forget him. I loved him so much, just because he was part of Don's family. Whatever my reason was, I loved him. I know if Brad was here, he would have put his arm around me protecting us. Now it is only me doing the protecting. The rain was coming down and it was getting cooler out. We were already into September and the weather changes fast in Oregon. It could be cold and then warm.

Sitting on the cliff

I went to the cliff taking my rifle and binoculars. I could see everything from where I was sitting. I could see the town from a distance. I even saw more with my binoculars. I tried to see what was happening and there was smoke which told me something was burning such as a building. I thought of Richard hoping he was safe. I was thinking and I heard Jack on his phone talking. He was in the back of the cabin. I was in the front sitting. He kept saying, "Yes, here is the address and come quick." I was wondering who he was speaking to. It wasn't my business, but it intrigues me. Then I heard footsteps and Jack came in the front. He was surprised to see me. Jack asked me, "How long have you been here?" I said, "Oh, I just got here." He smiled. I went back inside as I wondered about Jack and how strange he was acting today.

Jack is nervous

I was sitting in the living room talking to Melinda. Then Jack was going in and out the door. I looked at him as he smiled. I asked if we are under attack and he said, "No, I am just watching in case." I told him to yell if we are. He said, "I will." He went back outside, and Heidi thought Jack was crazy. I asked her, "How long has he been like this?" She said, "Since yesterday." I said nothing. I guess things were getting the best of Jack. I continued to sit and talk as it was teatime. Rosa brought over tea for us and a cake she made. I loved chocolate and so I had a small slice and drank my tea. Jack came inside and he saw the cake. I told him to stop being nervous and have cake. He said, "I have to watch my figure." I just stood there speechless. I was not sure what to make of him. His erratic behavior lasted the entire day and so I just watched and talked.

Can it be?

The following day it was hot outside and we were sitting in the back facing the stream. I could hear a lot of the people in the stream. I heard a vehicle coming in and since Jack was roaming, I was sure it was him. I was getting the sun as I heard footsteps behind me. I was hoping that Jack was finished with his craziness. Then I felt someone touch me on the shoulder. I turned around and I screamed. "Oh my God, what are you doing here?" It was Brad. He smiled,

"Hello Jennifer." I looked at Jack, "What is going on here?" Brad said, "I had Jack set up my death so you could realize that I did love you and I wanted to know if you really did too. Plus, I wanted to get help." I fell on my knees as everyone looked. Melinda fainted on the ground as Dora went to her. Grace went to Brad, "Is that really you Brad?" He said, "Of course Aunt Grace it is me." I wasn't sure if I was seeing things or dreaming. I asked Brad why he plotted all of this against me. He said, "Because of love. I love you so much and I wanted to work on my drinking. I found a drinking counselor in the area of Redding. I went to her and I am feeling much better. I am cleaned of alcohol." I stood up as Brad came closer to me,

"I missed you so much." I told him, "You put me through so much sorrow, I am not sure if I could accept any of this nonsense that you and Jack set up against me." Melinda was on the chair and she looked at her son, "Brad are you alive or dead?" He said, "Mother I am alive, and I never died." She got up and walked over to Brad as she hugged him. Everyone in the group was in shock and I think I was the worst case. Dora asked if I was alright. I asked if she knew all about this and she said, "Unfortunately I did." I looked at Tom, "You too?" He said, "I did." I laughed, "Well, that takes care of all the people I trusted. How many more knew of this?" The warriors also knew, and I thanked all of them for their deceitfulness towards me, especially allowing me to suffer. My daughters stood there as they felt bad. I told Brad, "If you think after this practical joke, I am coming back to you, you are nuts. I am done with all of you in this group." I went inside, got my suitcases and threw everything in the bedding of the truck. I put Clara in her car seat and Samantha along with Carrie went with me. Phyllis said, "I was not part of it, and so I am coming with you Jennifer." She got into my truck and I told her to get inside and so Samantha along with Carrie took their vehicles. I looked at Brad, "You are on your own Brad. Thanks for putting me through so much pain." I left him for good as the joke backfired to him and the others. I rode out of Cottage Grove as I wanted to get further away from all that played that joke on me. No wonder why Jack wanted to come here to be with us. It all shows now. I decided to ride until I would get out of the area.

Finding shelter

There was a house to our left on a deserted road. I wasn't sure where we were, but I did know that it was two hours away from Cottage Grove. I did not want to be bother with any of them in what they did to me. It was uncalled for and I was the one who went through the pain and suffering of losing Brad. There was a small abandoned house and we went inside. It was only five of us including my baby daughter. Samantha said, "This is nice." I said, "It will do for us." We settled down as we looked around and it had three bedrooms. Good for us. I didn't know where we were and so I went outside bringing in rations. We had enough to eat for a week or so. I told the girls, "We will go tomorrow and find a grocery store or something in the area."

Lebanon, Oregon

We all went out and took my truck. I found a sign that said, "Welcome to Lebanon, Oregon." We rode around for a bit and found a grocery store. I told Carrie, "Well here we are." We got out and Clara was with Samantha. We went into the grocery store and I put Clara in the seat of the cart. I told the girls to buy plenty of lunchmeat and whatever else. I bought Clara baby food and whatever else we needed. We had a lot of food and so I paid the bill and we put the bags in the truck. The town was quaint and so we found a luncheonette and decided to have a bite to eat. I locked the truck and then we went to have something to eat. It was a nice town and the people were friendly. We went into the restaurant and then sat down. It wasn't crowded, but the food smelled good.

Old Country food

The waitress welcomed us, and she gave us the menu and then told us the lunch special. I wanted to try chicken and biscuits, it just sounded old-fashioned. My daughters had their usual which was burgers and fries. I ordered Clara a hot dog and mac n' cheese. Clara was talking to me, "Mama I like dogs." I laughed, "I am sure you do honey." Samantha asked if I was alright. I said, "I am fine, just furious in what a lot of them did to me, including my husband." Carrie said, "I know mother that was wrong of him and them." I said, "I don't want to talk much about it because it makes me angry." The food arrived and we said our Grace to God. I cut up Clara's hot dog into tiny pieces and her mac n' cheese. We ate and it was delicious as it looked.

Adapting to my life

We stayed in this old abandoned house that was nasty looking outside, but nice inside. It was weeks that we were making it on our own. We had fresh water and electric. Since it was getting colder out, oh well we went to the shopping center to buy winter clothing. I bought new boots and a coat to wear. I also bough Clara a snowsuit to keep her warm along with a hat and mittens. We had plenty of food and clothing. I would go out chopping wood for the fireplace. I learned to be independent and to depend on God more. I didn't miss Brad or anyone. I knew I was divorced and happier in my life. I didn't need a man or anyone to help me. I read my bible each day and prayed more. When hard times hit, we were ready for them and we always found a solution. Every other day we would go into town to eat at the luncheonette. That was our treat to each other. The waitress knew us and would always welcome us with a smile. Then one day she asked my daughters if they needed a job. Samantha looked at me, "Well, I guess so." Carrie agreed and so she said, "I am the owner and I need good help." Samantha asked what kind of work and the owner's name Barbara was. She said, "I need a dishwasher and someone to help prep the food. You would both work Monday to Friday starting 7:00AM. They both agreed and I smiled as they said yes.

Winter sets

It has months since I last saw the group and Brad. I had the house warm and cozy while the girls worked. They were home by 3:00PM. Clara and I would rest during the day and so I would read or write. It was Friday and the girls were off for the next two days. They showed me their money and I congratulated them. I had dinner ready and tonight we were eating spaghetti and meatballs. I told them that I worked on the meatballs and the sauce was my own. Samantha admitted that the food smelled good. I told her to taste it and then comment. We sat down and ate. Clara was in her highchair and she enjoyed spaghetti. We ate and then we cleaned up. The wind was blowing, and I had the fireplace lit. I had enough wood for days and so I put another log inside the fireplace and then sat down. I had to give Clara a bath and so after my rest, I got up and gave her a warm bath. After she was finished, I put her to sleep. I myself took a shower and said good night to the girls. The fireplace was going, and I was warm in bed.

Snow is here

Barbara called the girls telling them that she was not opening the luncheonette due to the snow. It was snowing heavily, and I was afraid it was going to be a blizzard. I went outside and my truck was covered with snow. I let it go until it would stop. I went back inside as I brought in two logs and then I sat down. It was cold outside, and I told the girls to make sandwiches and so they did. I sat down with my sandwich and coke, ate, and then watched television. The meteorologist told the forecast and that it would stop snowing in a few days. The accumulation could be up to eight inches. That was not good. I didn't hear anything since we left the group. It has been three months and I was sure I would not hear anything from them. I couldn't care less and as far as I was concerned, everyone was involved. There was no way none of them knew what was happening. Someone knew something. How could they not see a body being taken out and not questioning? Even so if it was Brad, he was not dead. I could not believe that those warriors knew, especially Paul. I am glad that it was over with, and that I am here with my daughters. It was the best for me, and I know that we made it this far, and we could make it even further.

Going back to work

The girls went back to work and Phyllis along with me, well we played cards the rest of the afternoon while Clara played. Phyllis asked if I was happy. I laughed, "Of course I am and if you think not, you are wrong." She said, "I can't believe they did that to you." I laughed again, "I can." She said, "I did not pay much to it. All I heard was Brad is dead." I said, "Yeah, he was dead, and was everyone else." Then Phyllis asked if I had enough help in case of an attack. I said, "I am sure we will be fine. I am not worry." We played cards for a while and then before you knew it, the girls were home from work.

Home made

Phyllis made home made potato salad for dinner. I made home made burgers with a touch of cheese on top. I grated an onion to put on top of the burgers. When the girls came home, I had dinner ready. I asked how work was doing. Samantha said, "Actually it was quiet." I thought it would be. She then told me that news came on the radio about zombies in the area. I dropped my fork as I looked up, "You are kidding me?" Samantha said, "No, mother I am not." I went to the door to look out. I had to think what we had to do and that was to be on duty. I would go first and watch. I finished dinner and then I went to my truck as I got out the bazooka and flamethrower. I asked Phyllis if she knew how to fire the bazooka. She laughed, "Of course I do." I gave it to her as a present. Then I told the girls, "I will use the flamethrower." I was ready for them and they knew it. I swore those zombies followed me to bother my life.

Guarding

I was on duty for two hours before midnight. I would walk outside and watch and anything I heard; I would question. I walked around and nothing. I was not sure where they were seen or even near our direction.

I was almost over with my walk and so Phyllis came out to relieve me. I told her to keep checking outside. She said that she would. I went inside as I threw in another log to keep us warm. I was not ready for those damn creatures to attack. I wanted peace and I was afraid I was not going to get it.

Barbara calls

Barbara called to let the girls know that the zombies were in the area. I spoke to Barb and I asked her if she had extra help for us. She said, "I have plenty." She asked where we were living. I told her, "In an abandoned home in the mountain." I described the area and she knew. She said, "My God Jennifer, that is where they are, get out now!" I asked if she could meet me at the luncheonette.

She said, "Of course." I yelled to everyone, "Get your things now, pack up!" Phyllis asked what happened and I told her we are in the area of the zombies. She looked at me, "Oh my God!" We put everything in the boxes and right into the vehicles. There was nothing left. I put out the fire and I took Clara. We left the house and rode to the town to meet Barbara. As we were riding, there was a pack of zombies ahead of me. I stopped dead. I looked, "Oh know, they are here. Hold on Phyllis and onto Clara." I told her not to open the window and the girls behind me stopped. I quickly stuck my head out the window and told Samantha, "Zombies ahead. Stay in your cars." Phyllis asked what I was going to do. I said, "What I am best at." I closed my eyes, took a deep breath and I put the truck into drive releasing my foot off the break and then I charged right at them. I waved the girls to come and then I hit the bastards down and I could not go into reverse because of my daughters being behind me, and so I ran down what I could and left. I had damn blood and guts on my truck. I told Phyllis to hold Clara and keep her safe. She kept saying, "I am." I ran down the rest that was a few feet away from the first group. We kept going as I rode to town hoping the bastards will not follow us.

Getting out

We arrived at the luncheonette and the sirens were ringing. Clara was crying and I told her it was alright. My truck had blood over the grill and damn guts hanging. I was furious to see that, and the smell knocked me off my feet. We parked the vehicles running to the luncheonette. I banged on the door as Barb opened it. We ran inside as I told her to lock the door. She asked what happened. I told her, "We had a battle with them near my home." I sat down as Barb got us drinks. I was wiping my face as I was sweating. She asked if I was alright and I said, "I am." Clara was calmed, and I wiped her face as I drank my coke. Barb asked if I was used to fighting them. I said, "Yes, I lost my team and I am looking for new ones." She said, "Well you can use me and my husband." I asked if he would join the group. She said, "If it is to kill them, yes he will." I asked if she and him had weapons. Yes, was the answer and that was good. She said, "I will take you to my house which isn't far, meet Bob and talk." I said, "That is fine with me." Phyllis took Clara as we locked up the luncheonette and got into our vehicles. We followed Barb to her home and like she said, "It is not far from here."

Meeting Bob

I met Bob and he was a nice guy. Barb told him everything and he said, "I know." Barb explained to Bob about what was happening and what we needed to do. He got up and went to his weapons and pulled out his rifle. It was a high-powered rifle with a scope. He said, "I am ready." Barb got her rifle and I asked if she knew how to shoot it. She said, "Of course I do" So I had two more added to my group. Bob said, "How far are they away from here?" I said, "I am not sure, but if I was to figure it out, perhaps five miles." I told Bob, "It is best for us to wait and see." He asked why that would be. I said, "They may not even come this way." He asked how long I have been doing this. I said, "Longer than you think." Barb said that she would make dinner and asked Bob to show us our rooms. I offered her money and she said, "No, it is fine." Bob said, "We have extra rooms and to have company is our pet peeve." I went to my room as I put Clara down. She grabbed me, "Mama where is dada?" I said, "He is somewhere, but not here." I couldn't tell Clara that her father was a jerk in what he did again to me. I changed her diaper and I lied down for a while. Then Barb called us down for dinner and so we ate.

Keep watch

I told Bob and Barb we needed to be on guard every two hours or else we could wake up with a surprise. I took the first watch and I waited to see if they would come around. I walked around in the snow looking and listening and nothing. I owed myself to Barb for telling me about the zombies being in the area we were staying. If she would have never said anything, we would have been attacked without warning. I owed it to her. I wrote a check out that night for her and Bob. I thought they could use it, more than I could. I had enough money in my life and probably not enough time to ever spend it. I came back inside and sat in the closed in porch. I watched and nothing. When midnight came, Phyllis took over the watch. I told her there was nothing and that I checked around the house and it was quiet.

My gratitude

I put the check on their table so when she would serve breakfast, Barb would recognize the check. She came up to me asking what the check was about and I explained. In a few words, she saved our lives. She showed the check to Bob and he said, "Jennifer, you don't have to do this for us." I said, "I have enough of money. I am an attorney and I am what I am now, someone who slays zombies. I have no more life as an attorney, let me share it with you." Barb hugged me and so did Bob. Phyllis and the girls were smiling. We sat down to have breakfast and it felt good for someone else to make it for me. We had pancakes, eggs, bacon and toast. I had enough of coffee and that was my favorite. Barb said, "It is snowing out." Bob said, "I can see it." As I was eating my phone rang. I looked to see, and it was Brad. I excused myself as I went outside to speak to him. He asked how I was, and I said, "I am fine." He asked where I was in Oregon. I told him that he did not need to know. He said that the group moved to Dallas, Oregon. I said, "Well that is great for you." He said, "I am sorry that I did that to you, I really am." I told him, "I am sure you are, just like you were when you went with that woman." I hung up on Brad and I was sure that he would get over me. I went back inside as I wanted to scream. Barb asked if I was alright. I laughed, "Yeah, I am fine." She said, "Jennifer if you need to talk, you may with me." I said, "I am fine, just battling with my former husband." She said, "Oh, that is so familiar these days." I agreed. Clara ran to me and I picked her up. I asked if she had enough to eat. She said, "I had toast mama." I asked if she liked it. She nodded, "Yes." I kissed her. I asked Barb if I could give her a bath. She said, "Go right ahead. Let me give you a clean towel for the little one." So, she went upstairs with me and gave me the towel. I ran the bath for her, and I put Clara into the water. She loved the water and was playing. She splashed and the water hit my face. I told her not to splash to hard. So, I washed her hair and body. I let her play for a while and then I took her out wrapped in a towel. I took her in our bedroom and wiped her down. I got her dressed and dried her hair. I then combed it pretty and I kissed her. She said, "Mama I want my bottle." I told her that I would have to make her one. I took her downstairs and I made her a bottle. Samantha was talking to someone on the phone and then the question was asked to me.

Chris

Samantha was talking to her father and he wanted to come to us. I asked Samantha if he knew about the death and prank of Brad. She said, "My father was sitting with me and we knew nothing. The only thing we saw was a body in a bag. We didn't know anything." I asked where he was and she said, "On the highway alone with Cookie." I said, "Cookie, you mean she is going with Chris?" Samantha said, "I don't know mother, but I have to tell dad." I spoke to Bob and Barb about Chris and Cookie. They talked it over and said, "I guess we are going to need more people, sure." I asked if she could give directions to Chris. She said, "Sure Jennifer." Samantha gave the phone to Barb and so she gave directions. I asked to speak to Chris, "If you tell them where we are, I will never speak to you again Chris." He said, 'I swear Jennifer I will not." He hung up and came here two hours after alone with Cookie.

Arrival

Chris pulled up with his truck and out

he and Cookie came. I met them outside and I asked if any of them said anything and he said, "Nothing." I thanked him. Cookie hugged me and I introduced them to Bob and Barb. Bob brought them downstairs to extra rooms in the basement. I thanked them for their hospitality. Bob said, "What you have done for us, we owe something back." Dinner was almost ready, and Bob told Chris, "Well at least I have a man to talk to. Come on Chris, dinner is ready." Chris and Cookie came up and I wasn't sure if them two were dating. I had nothing against it, but I guess they made a good couple. I asked Chris how the group was doing. He said, "Paul is directing the group, and everyone is doing fine." I was glad. Chris told me that he brought the cannon and I laughed, "You didn't." He said, "I did." I thanked him. He asked if anything was happening. While at dinner I got the chance to tell Chris the story about how we got to Bob and Barb's house. In between Chris told me that it was not right what Brad did to me.

The news begins

The news was on and the newscaster warned us of a zombie invasion and a virus that they are putting upon us. Nothing else was told to us and that they would keep the community updated with more news. I looked at Chris, "What virus?" Chris said, "They must mean a virus from the zombies." I laughed, "That can't be or is that the reason why they are that way?" Chris said, "I am not sure, but I feel this is going to get worse."

Chris asked how many weapons we had. I said, "Enough." Bob heard and said that he had four rifles. I told everyone, "We need to prepare." Bob told Chris, "Come down to the shop and we will make Molotov Cocktails." Chris went with Bob and we sat upstairs as Barb kept the news on. Phyllis and Cookie were cleaning their rifles and then loading them. I looked at Clara, "You are my main concern." Phyllis said, "Don't worry Jennifer, I will take care of her for you." I thanked her as I told her that she was my main concern before my own life. Samantha looked at me, "Mother, you know we will all make it." I said, "I know we will, but this can turn nasty." We got our rifles ready and I had to think of what was going on now with us. My heart was broken, and I knew that Brad was a jerk to me.

Looking for survival

We had no hope on earth anymore. We only had God. Cookie asked if I was always a believer in God. I said, "No, I never even wore this cross around my neck." She asked what changed my mind. I said, "Right after I found Sara and what was happening in Los Angeles." She said, "I understand." Then I told Cookie that when my first mission was moving faster than I could handle it, we found a church and we went into it for safety. That is when I found Christ and turned to him. The reason why is because those creatures would not come near the church. That is when I changed." Cookie said, "Then it is best we stay in a church." I said,

"Yes, that would be a good idea for us, because we will be safe."

Survival is here again

I had no one to scout and so I went out with Phyllis. I took my binoculars and I rode around the area. I could see nothing. It was cold today and the weather was changing. I told Phyllis we had to survive all of this. She told me that it was the worse and I knew it. She asked what we would do if the zombies attacked. I said, "We fight them and move out." It was hard for all of us and so we did what we could. I was not happy, but I was sure to do what I could. Our area was cleared, as far as I could see. Then again, they could be in another part of the mountain and of course seeing them is obsolete. It started to snow, and we went back to the house. Barb had cups of hot cocoa for us and so I took my boots off and sat down. Cookie and Chris were playing with Clara. She was running around, and I told her not to disrespect others. She sat down, "Mama can I play?" I said, "Yes, but not running around." She came to me kissing me and I told her that I loved her. She said, "Me too mama." I hugged her and drank my cocoa.

Things slow down

Things were slowing down, so they say. The zombies were around, and the military was dispatched. So, we had the zombies on one side and the military on the other. It was unbearable. We had to be on the look out all the time. Still we had to watch. Barb wanted to open the luncheonette and couldn't. I was not aware of any closings, but there were a lot as told by Barb. We had to sit inside waiting for a battle. Bob said that the winter would be much brutal since we were in higher altitude. I said, "That is fine with me because we have enough time to plan and plot." Barb had a closed in porch that was quite warm. You could sit there and watch the snow or zombies to come. So, I would, that is watch the snow fall. I had numerous calls from Brad begging me to take him back, as I have not answered his calls. Why would I take him back in what he did with that woman and then fake his death? How stupid does he think this attorney is? If he would have been prosecuted by me, I would have made sure he would be in jail for life for a scheme that he pulled on me. I called the cell phone company changing my number. I had to do so, or I would be haunted by him for the rest of my life. I was done and finished. No more husbands, no more.

Scanner tells it all

Bob and Chris had the scanner plugged in for me. I had the volume turned up so I could hear. A stress call came in about 2:43PM. It was in our area and so there was a man stuck in his vehicle and could not get out. Chris was talking to him and asked his location. He found the location and said that he would be over. Bob said, "I can take you there Chris to help this man." I told them to be careful. They left and the snow was coming down and so we sat down watching the news and wondering what was next. We were bored and Barb wanted to go to her business and see how things were. I told her that we could do so, and she said, "Come on Jennifer, let us go." Phyllis came and Cookie stayed back with my daughters and we took my truck. I was not taking any chances and so we took our weapons. We rode to the luncheonette and the town was deserted. I parked in the front of the business and Barb opened the door and so we went inside. It was cold out and the snow was blowing in our faces. Quickly she locked the door turning the lights on. We went in the back to examine the area to make sure there were no surprises. Everything was fine. Barb said, "Come on Jennifer sit down, let me make us a sandwich." I told her that would hit the spot. I sat down and she was making a sandwich for us as she put a scoop of potato salad on the side with chips. I told her, "Well this looks like we are eating in a deli." She laughed. The sandwich was good and so we talked, and she said, "I can't believe how dead it looks out there." I said, "Yeah, dead, and we don't know what is dead out there walking around." She said, "That is true." We finished eating and so Barb made extra sandwiches for us to eat tonight and took the container of potato salad and bags of chips. I went to the door as I was ready to open it and there were a group of zombies standing in the street. I told Barb, "Don't move, they are out there." She looked carefully as I told her, "We can't go out there as yet." She asked if we should shoot them and I told her, "Not yet, wait on them, because if they are standing there, there may be a group of them somewhere else." We waited.

They must die!
We watched for a while and we stood behind the blinds. They went passed the luncheonette and then they stopped. I looked at Barb, "They must smell us." She was nervous. Then I told her, "We need to go to the back door and make sure it is secured. I told her not to make much noise and so we went back there. Luckily there was no back window for anyone to look in and so I went to the back door and it was secured. It was also a steel door which would make it tougher to bust inside. I put a crate of boxes in the front of it

securing the door. Then I went to the front again as I tried to see how many creatures were roaming near my truck. I told Barb, "We need to get out and into the truck and then I will take care of running them down. But we must run and not stop." She understood. She asked how we were going to lock the door. I said, "I forgot about that." I told her, "We will wait for them to move out of sight and then slowly go out." I waited and waited and then I made the move. I opened the door slowly and then came out to the front. I told Barb to hurry up and lock the door. We then went slowly to my truck as we got inside. I told Barb, "Lock the damn door now!" I turned the key, said a prayer and then backed up. The damn creatures were jumping into the back of the truck. I said, "You no good bastards!" I told Barb, "Hang on because this is going to be a ride of your life." I put my foot on the gas pedal full speed as my tires were spinning. I knocked down what was in front of me and then I reversed. I was smiling as Barb watched me. I said, "You are dead now!" I had to get them out of the bed of the truck, or they would make my truck ugly like them. I backed up and I kept rocking my truck and one fell out. There were two more and they had to leave. I then kept watching the back of the truck and I moved forward as I killed more on the street. I then backed up again and this time I went all the way back as I jerked the truck. They fell out and I crushed them with my big tires. I went forward as we went back to the house. My truck was covered with blood and guts.

Despair

I reached the house, and nothing was behind us. Barb jumped out of the truck with her bags and I sat there in despair. I wiped my face as I had wet snow melting on my hat. I took a deep breath and I got out. I took a step back as I looked at my truck and how dirty it was with matter hanging on the grill. Chris came out and looked, "Oh my God Jennifer, what happened?" I told him, "We ran into a group of them that was crazy as ever." He said, "It looks it. I guess you did your killings." I said, "You're damn right I did." Chris said, "I will ask Bob about cleaning the truck." I said, "Good luck." I went inside and I took off my wet clothes and I put on warm clothing. My feet were freezing and so I sat before the fireplace. Barb gave me hot cocoa and praised me for what I have done to save us. Bob congratulated me and I told him that I was used to doing all that I did. I went into the kitchen and there I saw a stranger sitting at the table. I said hello as I assumed this was the man that was saved. He said, "Hello, my name is Scott." He shook my hand as I said, "My name is Jennifer." He said, "I am the one who was stranded in the snow." I said, "Oh, okay, it was you." He smiled, "Yes, that was me." I told him it was nice meeting him and I went back to the living room to sit and relax.

Thanksgiving plans

We were in November and Barb said, "I believe we will be here until the winter ends. I have a turkey in our freezer and plenty of food." I said, "Well that will work for us." She said, "Yes, I think so." Scott was shy and didn't say much. I can only describe him as being shy, tall, handsome, and older. I didn't say much to Scott as I did not want any special greetings to me like Tom. I stayed away. Bob and Scott would talk, and I heard that Scott was single, and he lived in Dallas, Oregon. Bob asked how far he lived from us and he said, "Perhaps three miles out to the south." I was not expecting Scott to leave any sooner. We planned the dinner for Thanksgiving which was a week a way and Bob said, "I could start making the pies." Barb said, "That would work for us." I asked if I could do anything and she said,

"Yes. You could sit back and wait for Thanksgiving." I laughed, "I guess I could." So, Bob and Barb prepared for Thanksgiving as we helped.

Sirens

Sirens were ringing and echoing off the mountains and I knew it was because of the zombies, but where? Bob turned on the television and there it was, an invasion of the dead. The scientist was wondering where these zombies came from and then called it a strange virus. I looked at the newscaster, "A virus, wow, when did they figure that out?" Barb said, "If they have a virus, then that could mean we could get it." I said, "No, only if you are bit by one of them." Barb was scared and I told her not to worry and that we were safe. Bob said, "I am going out to see if there is anyone out there." Scott said, "Listen Bob I will go with you in case." They took their rifles and went to make their rounds. We sat there wondering when the zombies would attack. I knew they would be doing it soon. If they are in town, then they are headed towards us. The question is when and where. We all sat down to have a meeting. I told everyone, "We must make plans now or we will be running around like chickens without any heads." We had the weapons prepared, Molotov cocktails, ammunition, rations, food, rifles and the cannon. Chris said, "We have twenty-three cannonballs left." I told him that will be enough. I had the bazooka in which Scott was going to use. He was in the military and knew how to operate the bazooka. I thought well this is another Tom and I surely hoped he had no interest in me. I had no time for love or any of that. I had a daughter to protect, to raise, and a group to lead.

Thanksgiving Day

Barb and Phyllis had the turkey in the oven. Cookie and I were making the stuffing, pies, and salad. The girls were making odd things such as cookies. It was snowing and the fireplace was lit. I was grateful to Bob and Barb. They were such a good couple and they loved one another so much. I thought of Brad and how deceitful he was to me twice. I wanted to cry and then I said, "No Jennifer, you will not cry." Chris was setting the table with Scott and Bob was watching near the window. We all had something to do. The turkey would not be ready for at least four hours and so after I was finished, I sat down with a glass of wine. I brought in the bottles of wine I had. I knew that this was the last of the holidays and we knew nothing of what was ahead of us.

Sit down and pray

We sat down and prayed for everyone and everything. We were grateful to God for the food and everything we had to eat. We passed the food around as we took servings of the turkey, stuffing, corn, and gravy. I was overwhelmed in having this food because I haven't had a home cooked meal for such a long time. We sat there and ate. Barb passed the wine around and we took generous glasses of it. After dinner, we cleared the table and Barb made fresh coffee and put desserts on the table. We would help ourselves to the desserts. I had a piece of apple pie and that was delicious. It was made by Barb and I told her it was the best pie since my mother made them. She asked about my parents and I told her, "They passed away." She said that she was sorry. I said, "So am I." I tried not to think about them, but always at the holidays I do.

I need help

I told the group, "I need help, I mean scouts to go out and check the areas." Samantha said, "I can go out mother." I told her, "That is good, but it is dangerous." She said, "I know, but we must do what we need to do." I agreed and so Scott asked me what we needed. I said, "Scouts to go out and ride around checking the area for zombies or anything." He said, "I will do it for you." Then Bob said that he would help. I said, "Then you need to be careful, cautious, and armed." They went in Bob's truck as they had their rifles. We waited patiently for their return. After hours of waiting the news was not good.

They are here!

Bob ran inside, "Get out of here now!" I asked where they were. He said, "About a mile down the road." We got all our belongings together and then Bob locked the doors and we left in our vehicles. Phyllis and Cookie road with me and so I had company. I led the group out and I saw zombies running towards us and we had to get out or they would be all over us. The vehicles followed me out and so I road as fast as I could, but not easy on snow. I went through the back road and that was horrible. I had to put my truck into gear to get through the damn snow. After the turmoil I finally got out and we went on the highway. I wanted to get to the nearest business or something to avoid the fight. We finally arrived

Deserted!

Everything was closed. Everything was deserted. We had nothing to go on, nothing. The area was dead. No zombies, no people, nothing. I stopped to the side and I got out. Bob rolled down his window and everyone else came out. I said, "We have to find a place to stay because it is beginning to snow." Bob said, "We can stay at the luncheonette." I looked around, "Perhaps we could, but we had a battle there a few days ago." Barb said, "Then let us stay at one of the hotels." I got back into the truck and I went towards the hotel. I got out and I went to the door and it was opened. I called for someone and nothing. It was deserted. The guys came in and I asked them to go around and search. They did and then I stood there looking at the keys. Each one was marked with the room number and so I thought of us staying on the first floor. Cookie was holding Clara and I hugged my daughter. The guys came back and said everything was cleared. I gave out the keys to each and whoever wanted to share. Phyllis wanted to share with me, and I told her that she could. Chris locked the front door and closed off the lights. I took Clara with me to our room and Phyllis assisted me by helping me with our suitcases. I went inside the room and I put Clara down so she could walk. She went around looking and I told Phyllis, "Put on the television." She did and something had to be on. I went to tell Chris that he needed to get someone to help him bring in the rations from my truck. He asked how many and I said, "Ten should do." He went to get Scott and they went to the truck together.

Extended stay

We stayed at the hotel because the weather was cold and snowy. Being in December caused problems for us. Bob found the basement and put on the heat for us. It was operated by gas and that was good. Then we got brave enough and went into the kitchen looking for food and we found a lot of different varieties. There were slabs of bacon, roasts, chicken, and so much more. Barb fired up the ovens and started to cook. My daughters helped her and so did Bob. I asked if she needed any help. She said, "Get those pies out of the freezer and put some in the oven." So, I did, and we were going to have a feast in the evening.

The December blizzard

We ate good. Every day we ate good. There was so much food in the freezers and refrigerators. I told everyone that we were going to stay until the spring. If we were to leave, we would head into snow and lack of housing and food. I had to think of my daughter. We would walk around the hotel and sometimes we would change rooms so we would not be bored. Occasionally I would go out and scout by myself or sometimes, I would take someone. Nothing was around and the wind was blowing hard and so we would stay out for a while or until we could not see. Finally, a blizzard came over Oregon and it was cold. I mean it was cold. I was bundled up as I watched with my binoculars. When it got bad outside, I would go back into the truck to wait. I was sure the zombies were out there somewhere. I wasn't sure where, but they were. I was also sure that in the spring we would be seeing an invasion that will be bigger than what we had been involved with in the past.

Shopping

We were not far from the stores and so we went to the plaza to shop. It was days after the blizzard, and we took only one truck. Those who wanted to shop were doing it only for exchange of gifts. I wanted warmer tops and whatever else. I parked my truck and there were some vehicles in the parking lot. I was not sure if those cars were customers or what. We went inside and surprising the doors were opened. We went inside as I held onto my rifle as I wasn't sure who or what was around. There was no one around, no one. It was odd that stores were left opened. What threw me was that it looked as though there was a raid of some sort, you know looters. Phyllis and I were watching as Scott and Chris were behind us. We went into a clothing store and no one was around. I told everyone to get a bag and fill up. So, we did. I needed long sleeved tops and I took what I could and a few warm jeans. I told Phyllis, "I am going over to the children's dept." I then looked for Clara and I got her warm outfits and snow boots. I thought she would like them. I found a large bag and I went back to the women's dept. as I put what I could in the bag for the girls. All sizes would do.

Surprised

Scott and Chris took our bags to the truck. They came for us as we were looking in more shops. A few pairs of boots and hats, then we decided to leave. We went outside and I put my bags in the bed of the truck. I heard a noise and there were a group of looters behind us. The one leader came out and looked at us. He was tall, raggedy and nasty looking. I asked what his problem was, and I was sure he would become obnoxious. He had his pistol in his hand as he looked at me and then Phyllis. What he didn't know was that I had my hand on my rifle which was under my jacket. I was waiting for my chance. Scott was looking at Chris and I was hoping they would keep still. The thug looked at me again, "Well, you took our items and we want them back." I looked a him asking, "Is your name on the clothes?" He laughed, "Well, I have myself here a comical woman." I looked at him as I was not going to be defied by an idiot. Then he told his friends to get the bags and so they listened. They opened my tarp back and found not only bags, but rations and weapons. I had to stop them or else I would lose everything. I waited and as all three of them bent over into the bed of my truck, I opened my jacket as I took out my rifle and looked at Chris, Scott and Phyllis to shoot them. Our rifles were pointed at them as they tried to reach for their weapons, and we shot them dead as they fell on the ground. I looked at them as they lied dead spitting on them. We got into my truck and went back to the hotel with our packages and nothing missing.

Telling our story
When we returned, all of us were telling the story in what we went through. Barb congratulated me and said, "I like your style Jennifer." I told her, "It took a long time to get like this way." Everyone took what they

needed and happy at the same time. Phyllis and I took Clara and went back to our room. I hung up my clothes and I put on something warmer for Clara. I played with her for awhile and then Barb brought us dinner. I told Clara that she had to wash her hands and then sit on the floor with her plate to eat. We had meatloaf tonight and Clara enjoyed eating it. I sat on the bed as I turned on television. More snow was on the way and we were already in the third week of December. I told everyone that since a lot have not shopped for gifts, that they should give one another something that they owned to whoever. So, we drew names and that was the person we were to give a gift to. I had Carrie and so I had clothes that I got from the store. I knew her size and so that was no problem for me. Christmas was coming in three days and so we were ready to exchange our gifts. Barb said that in the freezer was a turkey and so she defrosted it and that was going to be our Christmas dinner with all the trimmings.

Gift of Life

I sat in my room as dinner was supposed to be ready around 4:30PM. I sat on my chair as Clara was playing and me thinking of Brad. Then I thought of Tom and how he was my hero so many times saving my life. I wanted to call Tom to wish him a happy holiday. I called his number and he answered. I said, "Tom, this is Jennifer." He said, "My gosh Jennifer, are you alright?" I said, "I am fine and you." He said, "I was hoping you would call me. I left the group because there was too much arguments with Jack. I am living in some cottage alone near Dallas." I told him that I was in the hotel staying on the strip in Dallas. He asked where I was and if he could come and see me. I said, "We are at the Dallas Hotel." He said, "I should be there shortly." He hung up and I could not believe it. I ran to tell Phyllis who was in the dining room setting the table. She saw me running as Clara was in my arms. She put the utensils down as she came to me, "Jennifer, what happened, zombies?" I said, "No, Tom is coming here to join the group." She said, "Well, that is good." I told her that I was going to meet him in the parking lot. I sat there waiting and soon after Tom showed up in his truck. He got out and he came to the door as I opened it for him. He came up to me, "Jennifer, I am glad you are alright." He hugged me. I said, "I am fine." He asked if he could come inside. I said, "Sure you could." He took the snow off his jacket and he saw Phyllis, "Hello Phyllis." Phyllis said hello to Tom, and I went behind the desk to get a key for Tom. I gave him the key, "Here is your room key." He looked at it, "Well, that was fast." I said, "Go ahead and put your suitcase away." He said, "Thanks." He walked to his room as I stood there.

The gifts

We gave one another gifts and Tom pulled out a box from his pocket to me. He said, "I have been holding this for a while and I thought

Christmas would be perfect to give it to you." I looked at him and I opened the box. It was a beautiful necklace. I asked for him to put it on my neck and so Tom did. I was not sure what it was all about, but I hugged him. I gave him a coat that I had when I went to that shopping center. He tried it on, and it fit him. Though Tom was tall and medium built, it fit him perfectly. We all sat down and had dinner and it was one of the best holiday dinners we had.

Bad news

I sat in the lobby of the hotel as I let Clara run and play. Tom was there and he said that he wanted to talk to me. I said, "Sure, what is up." He said, "Jennifer, I am sorry to say this, but when I left the group, Brad was dating Susan, and they were pretty serious." I looked at Tom, "Well, do I expect anything different from him?" Tom looked at me, "I guess not." I paid no mind to what was being said and I was furious inside, but that was strike three and Brad is now out. I went to my room and I told Phyllis what happened with Brad and she laughed. I told her that I was furious at first and then I thought that was his third strike against me. Phyllis asked if Susan was Brad's type. I laughed, "Who knows. I assume they found something in common." I told Phyllis that I didn't want to talk about him anymore and that life moves on. Phyllis asked if I liked Tom. I was honest, "Only as a friend and nothing else." I was not in love with Tom as I was before. What Brad did to me ruined my feelings for anyone. I didn't want to take any more chances on love again.

The truth

It was a cold bitter day. We were still at the hotel and we decided to stay until the spring, then we would move on. I was not too happy about staying, but it gave me a chance to plan where to go after this adventure. I sat down in the lobby and of course Tom joined me. He asked how I was doing. I said, "I am fine." He wanted to talk to me again. I stood up, "Tom, if it is about Brad or your feelings, I really am not in the mood." He said, "No, Jennifer, it is neither. I wanted to tell you who I am." I looked at him, "You told me a while back who you were and that is all that is needed to be said." He said, "No Jennifer. I am here to help you from danger. I am here to take you through this last mission." I looked at Tom, "What are you talking about Tom?" He said, "I am sent like Paul and the others." I stood up in shock, "You mean you are an angel?" He said, "Yes, I am. I am here to protect you and to help you find love again." I said, "Thank you for your help, but forget the love." He said, "No, you need to love everyone. Over the years you became bitter putting up a wall before you and others. It is time to let that shield fall." I got up, "I understand Tom, thank you for your help. I have to take care of my daughter." I got up and picked up Clara as I took her to the room where I sat down to think. I was not happy that Tom was an angel and I felt odd in how I felt for him. I just couldn't accept who he was and what. I wasn't sure if Tom was important in this mission or not.

Another day of snow

It was snowing and I thought to take a walk around the hotel. I put Clara's snowsuit on her, and I bundled up myself. Everyone was down in the kitchen to cook lunch and dinner. I wanted to go out. I was tired of being inside and plus I had to start my truck. Clara and I left as we went to my truck, and I started it with no problems. Clara wanted to go in the snow. I told her, "We will make snowballs together." I locked up my truck and I picked up snow to make balls out of them. I gave one to Clara and she threw it. I told her, "Well, you did that good." She laughed. We played for a while and then I picked her up as I walked around the parking lot. I saw that some of the stores were opened and so I decided to go back to my truck to ride over to the stores.

Nothing good

I told Clara that I was going to get out and put her in the stroller. One department store was opened, and nothing would stop me from doing this. I wanted to be out even though it was snowing. Clara had her snowsuit on, and I took her hat off and gloves. I took her stroller and so I put her inside as I went around the store. She looked at the different items as we went by. I asked Clara if she wanted a stuffed animal and she nodded. I looked at the stuffed animals and then I asked Clara, "Which one do you want?" She pointed to the one in the back and that was a tiger. I took it from the shelf as I gave it to Clara. She hugged it. I looked around and I saw a lot of toys and so I bought more toys for Clara. I didn't need anything and so I bought her toys and the tiger. I asked the clerk not to bag the stuffed animal and so I gave the tiger to Clara. She loved her. I took the bag and I left the store. It was snowing and so I told Clara that we were going back. It wasn't bad driving back, but the snow was coming down. Chris was at the door and he let me in as he took my bags. I had Clara and it was hard enough. I went to the room and Clara was running. I told her to stop and so she fell. There she was crying, and she hurt her lip. Barb and Bob came out and Tom. The rest were in the dining room.

Tom looked at Clara's lip and said, "Just some ice." He went downstairs to get ice and then he came back with the ice wrapped in a washcloth. I put it on Clara's lip, and she was crying. I told her not to cry and that the ice would make it feel better. I thanked Tom and he went back to his room. Phyllis came upstairs and asked what happened. I told her and she asked if Clara was alright. I told her that she was fine and her first accident. I took off Clara's snowsuit and she was sitting on the floor. I sat down as I made myself a hot cocoa and a sippy cup for Clara.

Moving fast

The winter was harsh. We were in the beginning of February and Oregon was brutal. The snow hammered us so many times that it was hard to get out. Tom would take care of our vehicles with Chris and Bob. I could not believe that Tom was sent by God to me. How could that be? I felt horrible that I fell in love with him. What did he think of me? I tried avoiding Tom and so I stayed in my room or I went down to the kitchen where food was being prepared. I took Clara downstairs with me and Samantha and Carrie were cooking with Barb. I smelled something good and I asked what was being cooked. Barb said, "Actually we are making cheeseburger and fries." I said, "Well that smells good." Barb asked if I was hungry. I said, "I am." She said that she would cut up a burger for Clara with a few fries. Clara was hungry and so was I. I told her to be patient and soon she could eat. Samantha asked how I was doing, and I told her that I was alright. After waiting, we finally sat down to eat. She sent Carrie upstairs to tell everyone lunch was ready. I told Carrie that the guys were outside. She went upstairs and I sat down with Clara ready to eat.

No life, no direction Phyllis sat down as we talked. She asked if I was ready for the spring. I said, "As far at the weather, yes, but as far as what is to come, no." She asked where we were going to go after this adventure. I told her, "I am not sure yet, but I am sure by March I will have a clear idea where." She asked if I would consider going to Nevada. I was not sure if that was on my agenda yet. We then talked about us and that I was getting older. She asked how old I was. I told her that I was now forty-three and climbing. She said, "I know that feeling. I am now forty-six." It was harder at times for me since I had many injuries to my legs and feet. I did tell Phyllis that we are going to come across a lot of zombies this summer and not only that, but also the military. She said, "I know this is going to be tough." I said, "I think we will be spending a lot of residency in building to get where we should go." She nodded, "I think that too." I told her my concerned was about my daughter and the group. She told me that we will be fine. I knew we would be and that we had a good group. She asked if I missed Jack and them. I said, "I do, but I cannot take Brad and going back. I heard from Jack a few weeks ago and he pleaded me to return." I told him I wouldn't. Brad struck out three times with me and there will never be anything with us again.

Scouting alone

Phyllis took care of Clara while I went out to scout. The sun was out today, and it was cold. I was glad that it was not snowing. I wanted to go over to the mountain and watch. There was a clear view for me to see and so I had my binoculars to see. What was bad about the snow was that I could not see much better if anything was around. I had my rifle and machete just in case. It was not easy sitting on wet snow. I did it, because of the position I was now in. I looked all around, and I thought of moving my position, so I did. I went to the opposite side of where I was sitting and then my view was much better. I then looked and then my eyes were glued.

The noise

The noise I made brought the attention of the zombies below me. They looked and made an awful sound as they ran. I knew they were coming after me. I got down from the boulder I was sitting on and ran as fast as I could to the hotel. I stopped to look and nothing. I banged on the door and then Scott opened it for me. I screamed, "Damn it, there is a group of zombies coming this way, get your weapons." I yelled it out and I told Chris to get to the cannon. Tom got the bazooka and so we waited. I went outside and went behind my truck to watch. I then saw movement and I told Chris to position the cannon to the right about 45 degrees. He did. He made it a point to watch as I did and had binoculars too. I watched with him as the group was standing on alert in the lobby near the door. We waited.

The Fight

Both Chris and I saw them running towards us and that is when I flagged the group to come out and shoot them. Chris put a cannonball into the cannon and shot it right into the group. Tom had the bazooka firing it on the next group behind them killing them. The body pieces were shattered and falling over the area. We shot them, and I was not happy that we did not have many weapons, but we fought with what we had. Chris kept shooting them with the cannon and none were coming to us. Luckily there were not many, but enough to cause grief. After battling them for some time, we finally put down our weapons as we cased the area. We went forward as we checked to see if there were any alive. Most were ripped apart by the cannon and bazooka. So, we went as far as we could and then we went back inside the hotel. Chris of course covered the cannon and he went back inside with us. I told him that I was pleased with his ability to shoot the cannon and he smiled. Tom did a good job on the bazooka and so we all went downstairs to sit down and get a drink.

Three cheers

We went downstairs and Cookie had Clara for me. I asked if they were both alright and she said, "As safe as could be." I thanked her for taking care of my daughter and herself. She asked what happened out there and I told her the story. I was out of breath as I sat down. Barb poured us drinks and so we drank and talked. I told everyone that they all deserved three cheers for their ability to fight. Bob said, "They are suckers those creatures and I am concerned about us when it gets warmer." I said, "I know. Soon we are going to sit down and go over what we need to do in the spring and summer." Barb said, "Maybe we could return back to the mountain." I said, "Perhaps." I was honest telling Phyllis that I didn't have a plan yet, but I will.

Tom talks

Tom told me that he heard from Jack and I asked how everything was with him. He said, "The warriors left, and the group is doing alright." I asked where the warriors went. Tom said, "Jennifer, you know where they went. It is evident." I thought, "I know Tom. It was because I was not there to lead the group. They left and went back to God." He nodded, "Yes, and I am the only one left." I was upset and I told Tom, "I didn't want them to leave and it is my fault." Tom said, "No, it was your choice and that is why I am here. Now I have instructions what I must do for you." I looked at him, "I understand and still my life is a mess." Tom said, "Jennifer, there is so much to come and happen, and you must be prepared." I told Tom that I was and what would happen would not surprise me. I thanked Tom for his information. I was about to walk away and then Tom called me, "Jennifer, there is more." I looked and asked, "What more can it be?" He said, "Brad left the group and is headed here." I looked at Tom, "How did he know?" I looked at Tom, "It was you that told them and now I have to go through it again with Brad." Tom said, "You must realize that Brad has a daughter and her name is Clara." I took a deep breath and went to my room where I sat to think. Phyllis asked me what happened. I told her, "Brad is coming." She looked at me, "Ah oh."

Don't remind me

Tom told me that Brad did not know where we were. I told him, "Well this area is large, so what is he going to do, go place to place searching for me and Clara?" He said, "Jennifer, you are going to have to be strong about this and not give in." I said, "I am not. We are divorce and he struck out three times with me. I don't love him like I did." Tom agreed and said that I still needed to stay strong. The good thing about this is that it was snowing. We were only in the beginning of February and the snow was heavy. I was sure that Brad would be somewhere and not near us. I thought of the vehicles being seen and I was not sure what to do about that. So, I asked Tom, "What should we do about the vehicles?" He said, "Nothing. You are safe until the spring." I took a deep breath, good for me. By then we will head out of this area into another place that would be further away from Dallas." Tom agreed. I went to the lobby as I looked outside, and it was snowing. More then I could handle. I was sure that Brad was somewhere on the other side of town and not near here.

Walking in the snow

A few of us went out to walk. It was snowing and the visibility was not good. We went around the area as I wanted to take Clara, but I was cautions of her getting sick. It was cold out and I could not take the wind. Barb, Cookie and I went out and we needed to get out for a while. Tom stood by near the lobby to let us back inside. I tried looking through my binoculars and I could see nothing but snow. Cookie asked me, "What are you looking for?" I said, "Zombies and Brad." She said, "Brad, is he in town?" I said, "I am not sure, but I am not taking a chance." Barb said, "Don't worry if he gets crazy, we will take care of him fast." I laughed, "I am sure I can take care of him." We continued to walk and there was no one around, at least that I could see. We turned around and went back to the hotel. The area that we could see looked like a war zone. No one was around, cars parked all over, and an eerie wind blowing. We got back at the hotel and no sign of Brad. I was praying that he got lost somewhere, but knowing him being an Oregonian, he knows his way around the state.

Planning ahead

I sat in the conference room looking at my map. I had my coffee and the blinds were drawn. It was snowing and so I tried to make the best of my decision. I looked to see where we were and where we could go in a few weeks. The furthest we could travel was to go to Salem, Oregon. It is bigger and the capital. I measured with my compass and damn it, it was only fifteen miles away. That was not the problem, what was the problem was that we were not far away enough. I had to take it slow or just do the nine hundred miles and go back to Los Angeles. I was stuck and I had to think. I thought to ask everyone before going ahead. I knew that the zombies would be out in the spring and summer and so we had to do something. Then I had to think of Brad and since he knew Oregon from the back of his hand, well I had to think like him. That was not hard for me to do. I looked to see if it was wise to stay in Oregon.

One step ahead

I called a meeting with everyone during dinner time. I had to find out what they thought of my plans. Bob said, "I think Salem is wise. We need to take baby steps on this journey and feel around us what is happening." I agreed with him. I told him that I would work on a back up plan in case it would not work in Salem. Barb said, "Jennifer, Salem is large enough to go any where and so we have a lot to go on." I agreed with her and so Salem it was. I told them, "If we are attacked, then we will move inland and escape." They agreed. I asked how the weapons were and everyone said, "Up to date." Good. I looked at the map and I said, "If by chance we are attacked or pushed by looters or anything, we will move near Ice

Mountain." Barb laughed, "Hey we used to take the kids there." I asked if it was nice. She said, "Back then. I am not sure how it is now." I said, "Well, this area looks large enough and we could find some kind of shelter there." We had our plans intact and all we needed now was the spring.

Brad is here

The snow stopped and so I went outside scraping the ice off my windshield and taking the snow off my truck. Everyone was inside playing cards and eating. I needed a breath of air. I was scraping the ice off the windshield and then I turned around and there was Brad. He looked at me as I did not recognize him. He had a beard and mustache and his hair was longer. He smiled, "Jennifer, how are you?" I looked at him as I smiled, "You never do give up." He said, "No, because I love you, but you have been too bold to understand my heart." I finished my truck and I asked why he was looking for me. He said, "First, my daughter, and second you." I looked at Brad, "I cannot take you back because of you." Brad took his cigarette and threw it on the ground as he said, "I am sober since you left, I have changed, and I am here now with you." I asked what about Susan. He laughed, "She was just company and nothing and if you don't believe me, ask anyone there." I invited him inside to see his daughter. He took the snow off his hat and combed his hair back. I didn't want to tell Brad that I still loved him, and I couldn't look at him without smiling. I took

Brad to my room as Phyllis was there. She stood up and welcomed Brad. He said hello to Phyllis and then he went over to his daughter. He picked her up, "Clara, you grew. Daddy is now here." Phyllis smiled and I looked at her as I nodded. She left and told me she went to see the others.

No way

Brad sat down as he took off his jacket. He put his hat back on and looked at me, "Well, you are still beautiful, and I missed you." I laughed, "Come on Brad, I divorced you and I have nothing for you here." He said, "Then I am not here to argue. Let me get myself a room here and at least I am here to see my daughter." I agreed and so I took him downstairs to get him a key. He went to his room and I went back to mine.

I was not thrilled he was back, but I accepted it. I had no time to argue and I thought of Clara. Phyllis returned and asked if I was happy. I said, "No, I am not, but I don't want to argue either." I sat down and I was sipping my cocoa. She looked at me, "You do love him." I said, "Love has nothing to do with him Phyllis, but when someone fakes their death to get my attention, then we have a problem." She agreed. It was almost dinnertime and I went to tell Brad and he came with me as he held Clara. We went downstairs and everyone who knew Brad said hello, and those who didn't I introduced him. I told Brad to put Clara in her highchair and so he did. I sat down as Barb passed the food around. Brad of course sat next to me smiling.

The bad news

Brad was sitting in the lobby as he was smoking. I put Clara down and she ran to Brad, "Daddy." He put out his cigarette and picked up Clara. He looked at me, "At least she loves me." I told him to knock it off. He put down Clara and asked me to sit down. I sat down and he told me, "During these months I lost you and my mother. She passed away shortly after you left. Her heart gave in and Dora could do nothing. My aunt was upset, and she stayed with the group." I started to tear up and I couldn't believe it. I told Brad, "I am so sorry Brad." He said, "I went through a lot while you left. I became sober because I had to change. My mother left and now I have only my daughter." I told him that I did love him, but I didn't want any more relationships. He said he understood and asked if he could stay to help. I said, "Yes, you may." He thanked me. Then he asked if any of the stores were opened. I said, "Some." He asked where they were, and I told him. He put on his coat and said he would be back. Brad got into his truck and left. I was not sure if he really left or just went to the store.

The smile that shined Brad returned and he had bags. He took out toys for Clara and gave them to her. I thanked him. He said, "I can't make up what I lost with her, but I surely can try." Then he gave me a box of candy. I smiled, "Thank you." He smiled. He told me that he would be going back to his room. I thanked him again and then I went to take a shower. I was tired from doing nothing. Clara was playing and Phyllis asked why I wouldn't want to give Brad another chance. I said, "Because I am divorced from him, and secondly, I don't have the love I once had for him." She looked at me, "I guess that is a good answer." Then she said something about Tom. I said, "You know about the warriors?" She nodded. I continued, "Well, Tom is the same." She looked at me, "You must be joking?" I said, "No, I am not." I explained to Phyllis that I am not interested neither in Tom nor anyone. I had enough of marriages and love. Whatever is in my heart remains and that is all I have. I kept watching Clara and she was playing with her toys that Brad bought for her. She smiled, "Mommy, toys."

Heat goes off

We lost our heat. It was cold in our room and so I told Phyllis to make sure to keep Clara inside the bathroom. There was an electric heater and it was on. I put on my jacket and went to Brad's room. He asked what happened. I said, "Something went wrong with the heat." He asked where the furnace was located. I told him, "I guess downstairs." He got his toolbox out of his truck and I took him to the basement. In between Bob came with us as he was talking to Brad. The basement was enormous and so they found the furnace. Bob looked as Brad did the same and the pilot light was out. Brad said, "I have the right tool that will light the furnace." Bob said, "I am happy you came along."

He said, "I wish everyone would feel that way." Bob looked at me. I shook my head as I waited for the furnace to heat up. It was on and Bob thanked Brad as I did the same. We went upstairs and Bob told everyone, "The heat is on." It took an hour or so before we got back to where we should be. Brad told me, "That furnace needs to be cleaned out and I hope it stays that way for a few more weeks." I said, "I hope so." I invited Brad inside to see Clara and I think I was making it an excuse so I could see Brad. Brad was on the floor playing with her. I sat on the bed watching and Phyllis was watching the news. Then suddenly, she said, "Oh my, look, looting!" I looked at the news and there was looting. Looting was being done by groups in

Dallas and warnings have gone out about not going out. Brad said, "Shoot them down." I said, "No, only if we are attacked Brad. I don't want anyone hurt." He said, "I won't do anything nonsense." I thanked him. He asked how long we were staying here and then where to. I said, "As soon as the spring sets in and we are going to Salem." He said, "I guess that is a smart move." I looked at Brad and he had so much hurt in his face. I felt bad that he lost his mother through all of this. Melinda was such a nice woman, bit older, but nice. My heart broke for Brad because he went through enough, more than Don did. I went up to Brad telling him that I was sorry for all he has gone through. He looked at me, "I know, so am I. Even though we can't be back together, at least I am here with you and my daughter." I said, "Yes, I agree." That night it snowed and after dinner I took a warm bath to relax. Clara went to sleep, and Phyllis kept her eyes on the news. I wondered what Brad was doing and so I got dressed and I went to see him.

Me too, you too

I knocked on Brad's door and he answered. He asked if I was to see him or to ask questions. I laughed, "The first one." He opened the door. I said, "I want to see how you are doing." He said, "I am doing well. Just having some chips and looking at television." I asked if I was bothering him. He said, "Not at all." Then he asked about Clara and I assured him that she was sleeping and Phyllis watching her. I sat down and I asked

Brad about the group. He said, "They were doing fine. They were disappointed that you left them and felt betrayed by you." I said, "I have not betrayed them, I left because I was disgusted over what was happening." Brad understood and said that I needed to understand that he loved me. I told him that I knew, but that I changed. He looked at me, "I think you are lying because if you did not love me, you would not be here sitting with me." I looked at Brad and said nothing. Then he put his arms around me kissing me and I didn't turn it away. He hugged me, "I love you so much and you were to me the moment I met you." I said, "I can't Brad, I can't. I have to go." He said, "Hey, I have protection if you decided we could get back together."

I said, "It is not about that." I told him to take care and I left. I was not myself and I wanted to stay with him, and I refused. I didn't want to restart something that was not there.

Rethinking the route

I went into the conference room alone with my map. I only had a few weeks before spring would begin. We had to leave here because in a few weeks we would be running out of food. I did not want to go out of Oregon and into Nevada and if I push it far into Salem, then I would be nearing Nevada. I looked at the map and prayed. Then there was a knock at the door. It was Tom. I told him to sit down and so he did. He asked what I was deciding on. I said, "Well, I wanted us to go into Salem, but I am not sure if that is a right idea." He looked at the map, "You are looking at the Cascade mountains." I said, "Yes, I was." He said, "That is fine for two reason, food and water." I said, "Sure there is plenty of streams, and food, well we would have to hunt or find food." He said, "I understand. So, you want to know if that is a right choice." I said, "Yes, I need some lead way Tom." Tom stood up, "The answers are there for you Jennifer. They always have been, but you have been avoiding them." I looked at him, "What choices?" He said, "The choice where to go, what to do and whatever else you have been questioning God on." I took a deep sigh, "Perhaps I have." Your answer is there, and the Cascades is good for hiding and the zombies are mostly in the open area and not in the mountains. In fact, they descended from the mountains and no longer can go back." I asked Tom, "Why is that?" He said, "Because God will not allow the evil to return. These creatures are a punishment against the evil wickedness of the earth. They will soon go away, but also the inhabitants of the earth." I looked at Tom, "Whoa, we are going off the topic." He said, "I am sorry, and yes go to the Cascades instead of Salem." I said, "Then that is where we will go." I asked Tom, "When do you go back?" He said, "When this is finished." I asked when that might be and he said, "When the end of the world comes." I told him that we had work to do. He smiled, "That is for sure."

Telling everyone

At dinner again, I told everyone that I made a revision of our plans. I said, "We are going to leave here in the spring heading towards the Cascade Mountains in Oregon." Brad smiled, "My homeland." I looked at Brad and then Barb asked if we were going to stay in the mountains. I said, "We will see what happens, but I am sure that we will be alright." Brad was sitting next to Barb and Bob asking if they were from Oregon. They both nodded and Barb asked Brad the same. He said, "Born and raised in Portland." Barb greeted Brad and winked at me. Brad just as Barb and Bob had an accent that was different. Brad was the type to have jeans and tee shirt on and his hat. He wore cowboy boots just as Al and Jack did.

It was a tradition. I tried to get back on the subject and not on being a native of Oregon. Everyone agreed and so we waited in which we had four more weeks for spring.

Weather improving
The weather was improving. Still there was enough snow on the ground and on the hilltops. Brad said, "Sometimes it takes time to melt." I knew that and so I asked him if he ever climbed the mountain. He said, "No, never was interested." I told him that he was the type to do so. He said, "Not really." Clara was playing in the lobby and I went to the door. The snow was melting slowly and there were piles of water around. Brad took his hat off and combed his hair back. I asked when he decided to grow his hair. He said, "When I

stopped drinking." I nodded. We sat there and soon Bob and Barb came down to see what was happening. Before you knew it, everyone was coming down. Brad was talking to Chris and Bob. Barb asked if Brad and I were married for long. I said, "As old as Clara is added with one month." She looked at me, "How old is Clara?" I said, "She is now fifteen-month-old." Then she wanted to know why we broke up because we make a nice couple. I laughed. She asked why I was laughing. I said, "For all the reasons." Barb said, "You should know the things I went through with Bob and we finally put everything to the side and stayed together. We have three beautiful children and I never would regret staying with him." I said, "Brad did a lot to me." She said, "I understand, but none of us are perfect. Forgive him and move on." I had a knife stuck in my heart and so I decided to pull it out and give Brad another try.

One more

I spoke to Brad that night as I told him that I would give him another chance, and if he messes up this time, I will leave him permanently. He said, "I understand, but there will not be another time." So, I asked Phyllis to babysit Clara for the night and I spent my night with Brad. I made sure that he used protection and he did. I did not want to have any more babies or lose any. We agreed on that. He asked if we were really divorced. I said, "I am not sure. Los Angeles has been closed for so long and still a lot of the offices are down. I am assuming no we are not." He said, "That is good, because I love you and I want to stay married to you." I told him that I agreed. We stayed up for hours and hours and then finally we fell asleep as I laid in his arms. I wanted to leave, but then I said, "No, forgive him." I was still not sure about that woman and why. I let it go and I forgave Brad. Something that I could not do before. I fell asleep and then I woke up at 6:00AM. I was tired and so I took a shower as Brad was sleeping and then I got dressed and went to my room where Phyllis and Clara were sleeping. I looked for clean clothes and I went to get dressed and then doing my hair and makeup. I wanted to look nice for Brad when he wakes up. After I was finished, Phyllis was getting up and asked how I enjoyed myself. I said, "After such along time, it was good." She smiled. Then I saw Clara getting up and then standing in her playpen. She kept saying "Mommy." I went over picking her up. I asked if she was ready for breakfast. She nodded and so I checked her diaper. I told her that after breakfast she was going to have a bath and get dressed. She was smiling and then asked, "Daddy here." I said, "He will be." I went to my purse and I took out my wedding ring as I put it back on my finger. I noticed that Brad had his on, and I assumed he never took it off. Phyllis was up and asked if I would rather have Brad come to my room. I said, "No, I will take what I could over there with Clara, and you could stay here. She agreed and so I packed.

I do

Clara ran into the room and Brad was dressed and he stretched out his arms, "Come on little one." She ran right into his arms and he picked her up swinging her. Brad asked if I wanted to go have breakfast. I said, "Come on, let us go downstairs." He held Clara and then my hand as we went downstairs. Brad kissed me, "I do love you." I told him that I loved him. He looked at Clara, "Mommy loves me." She smiled. Then I asked Brad, "Did you ever take off your wedding ring?" He said, "Never. I knew someday we would be back together." I smiled. He saw I had my wedding ring on, and he said, "I know you didn't, but you never discarded it and that is what matters." We kissed and then sat down to eat.

Chris and Cookie

Cookie was talking to me about how Chris liked her. I asked how serious and she said, "Not too, but it could get there." I congratulated her. Cookie was lonely and so was Chris. They both were older than what we were many missions ago. I asked Cookie if Chris asked her out yet. She said, "He has, and we are waiting to go out when the weather gets warmer. I told her that we will be leaving in three weeks. She said that she could not wait. I was happy for both and I could see the happiness in both of their faces. I wondered if they could see any happiness in my face. I was happy that I was with Brad again, but always in the back of my mind I had doubts. It still bothered me when he played dead and let me suffer for so long thinking he was gone. My emotional distress that I suffered for so long thinking he shot himself. Then a few of them knew that he was playing dead, that is when I decided to leave the group.

Questioning Brad

That afternoon I questioned Brad about why he played dead. He laughed, "That is an odd way of putting it." I looked at him, "Then let me rephrase myself, why did you fake your death?" He cleared his throat and said, "Because I wanted to see if you loved me enough to wish me back to life." I stood up and looked at Brad, "You bastard, you did that to me hoping to find out how I truly felt. How could you Brad when I suffered so much with emotional distress? You made me suffer so much as I was ready to have a breakdown." Brad looked at me, "I am sorry Jennifer. I really am. It was my fault and I admitted to it. Please, I am sorry." I picked up Clara, "You don't deserve me ever." I went to the room as I gathered my few things and went back to where I was with Clara. Phyllis asked what happened and so I told her. She said, "That is cruel of him to do that putting you through suffering." I said, "Yeah, and I almost fell for his nonsense. I love Brad, but no. I cannot be with him like I was and last night was wrong of me." Phyllis said, "Did he wear protection?" I said, "Yes and thank God he did. I don't need another child." Phyllis said, "Then you are safe. Do what you feel is right. I know I wouldn't go back to my husband if he did that to me." I told her that most wouldn't. That day I decided to keep Brad out of my life.

The weather warms

We were in March and the snow melted and so we were ready to leave in a few days. I told the guys to pack what we could take for food and drinks. They did and we were ready to leave in two days. I thought of where to go and perhaps the Cascades was not the answer. I was not happy with Brad around, but to keep peace, I kept him with me. He was not happy that I did not want him back with me. He gave up asking and I was glad he did. The day before we were going to leave, he said that he loved me and accepted that I didn't want to be married to him. I told him, "That is great, and don't forget the reason." He said, "How could I when you remind me every other day." I packed my clothes and I put the suitcases in my truck. We had our last meal and we went to sleep.

Leaving Dallas

The sky was blue, and it was warm outside. There was still snow on the ground but melting. The mountains still had snow caps and perhaps melting in a few weeks. Phyllis sat with me watching Clara. Everyone was in their vehicles and Brad was behind my truck. I didn't pay much to him and so we left the hotel. We spent So many months there as it was time to leave. I followed the sign to Salem and so it was only twenty minutes to arrival. I wasn't sure what was waiting for us in Salem, but I did know that it was somewhere to try,

and if it is invaded by zombies or looters, then we leave. I knew that this was not going to be a vacation of any sort, but an escape until I was sure where to go.
R.g. Myers
April 2020